He took a closer look. The young woman's olive skin glistened in the sunlight, and her long, dark hair, though tangled and dirty, still caught his eye. Her deep brown eyes seemed to speak to him. This girl, whoever she was, was a knockout. A mess, but a knockout. She nodded, and her gaze shifted downward. Suddenly she came to life, her eyes widened in fear. "Oh my goodness! I need to get back in there." She struggled to rise to her feet.

"What?" What could possibly be so important?

"I left something in the Dumpster," she explained. "Something really important. I need it. Now."

JANICE THOMPSON is a Christian author who resides in south Texas with her husband and four daughters. Her entire family is active in their local church and in inner city missions. They spend much of their time working with Houston's homeless community. Together, they hope to make a difference by bringing the love of Christ to a generation of young people who simply need a helping hand.

Books by Janice Thompson

HEARTSONG PRESENTS
HP490—A Class of Her Own

Angel Incognito

Janice Thompson

Heartsong Presents

To Mary Anne.
You have found your identity in Christ, and it has birthed in you a
passion to reach the homeless with God's love. You are truly an angel.

To Kim and Martin Dale of YWAM/Houston, Joe Williams,
Turning Point Ministries, and members of CFC—you all encourage
me to want to do more to reach the "unreachable" ones. Together, we can
help them discover their true identity—one that can never be stolen.

A note from the Author:
I love to hear from my readers! You may correspond with me
by writing:

Janice Thompson
Author Relations
PO Box 719
Uhrichsville, OH 44683

ISBN 1-59310-056-6

ANGEL INCOGNITO

Our mission is to publish and distribute inspirational products offering exceptional value and biblical encouragement to the masses.

All scripture quotations, unless otherwise indicated, are taken from the HOLY BIBLE, NEW INTERNATIONAL VERSION®. NIV®. Copyright © 1973, 1978, 1984 by International Bible Society. Used by permission of Zondervan Publishing House. All rights reserved.

All of the characters and events in this book are fictitious. Any resemblance to actual persons, living or dead, or to actual events is purely coincidental.

PRINTED IN THE U.S.A.

one

"Angel, I don't know any other way to say this, so I'll just say it. You're simply not cut out to be a reporter. You don't have what it takes."

"But—" Angelina Fuentes's eyes filled with tears as she stared into the stern face of KRLA station manager, Mr. Kurt Nigel.

His expression remained unchanged. "No buts." He paced across the plush Los Angeles office and spoke with fervor. "We've given this several months, and you've made little improvement. To be honest, you're just too, too. . ." The older man snatched a glass paperweight from his untidy desk and rolled it around in his palms. His gaze shifted to the ground as he shrugged in defeat.

Angel sighed and pushed a strand of her long hair behind her right ear. "Go ahead and say it," she whispered. "I can take it."

"You're too soft." Mr. Nigel looked up with a determined expression. "When we hired you for this position you told us you had a tough side, but we just haven't seen it. Everything about you is, well, frankly, sweet." He dropped the paperweight with a thud.

Angelina lowered her head and fought back tears as the wayward hair slipped from behind her ear again. "I've tried. I really have." She twisted the strand with her index finger then pressed it back into place once more.

"Being sweet is nothing to be ashamed of." He patted her on the shoulder—his first attempt at kindness. "But reporting is a tough line of work and calls for tough people. People who can be mean. Nasty. People like me."

Angel gasped. "Oh, Mr. Nigel, you're not mean and nasty. You're one of the greatest men I've ever known." Her words were genuine, free from manipulation.

Her boss paced the room, clearly frustrated. The frown lines on his forehead deepened as he spoke. "See what I mean? You can't even be rough on me, and I deserve it more than anyone. Here I am, in the middle of firing you, and you compliment me." He shook his head, and the three hairs on top shifted slightly. "You're not making this any easier, I might add."

"Is that what you're doing? Firing me?" Angel suddenly felt the weight of the conversation bear down on her. He couldn't be firing her. She had only worked at KRLA a short time and hadn't even had a chance to prove herself yet. She needed time.

"Yes, if you'll let me. I'll even add a 'please' and 'thank you' if it will soften the blow a little." He grinned.

The lump in Angelina's throat wouldn't allow her to respond. She simply couldn't lose this job. The Lord had led her here. Surely He had a plan. She trusted Him completely, though her knees wobbled a bit at the moment.

She swallowed hard, but the lump refused to budge. To lose this job would be too devastating. Her struggles through college had been hard enough, but the transition from student to employee had almost sent her reeling. For weeks she had applied for positions and prayed for open doors. When the call came from KRLA, she felt confident she had heard the Lord's voice.

The station wanted a hard-hitting reporter. She had vowed to be tough from the beginning. She needed to remain just as tough right now—inside and out. Angel took a deep breath and stared squarely into Mr. Nigel's full, round face. He would change his mind. He had to. She opened her mouth to speak, but he cut her off before she began.

"You're a tiny little thing." He looked her over, lips pursed.

"Petite, sir," she corrected as she stretched to full measure. "Five-foot-one is nothing to be ashamed of. I'm taller than my mother and both of my grandmothers."

"Petite. Short. Whatever. And you've got those big brown puppy-dog eyes."

"Excuse me?"

"I guess what I'm saying here is this: From all outward appearances, you don't fit the mold of the tough reporter type. I was willing to give you a chance, thought maybe I'd find a bundle of energy packaged in that tiny little person, but—"

"Oh, I am, Mr. Nigel, I am!" She seemed to come alive with the words. "You just haven't seen me in action yet."

"That's putting it mildly."

She forged ahead. "I can do this job. I've trained for it. I'm determined. I just haven't found the right story yet. You'll see, sir."

He stared at her with cool gray eyes, undaunted.

"Please, Mr. Nigel."

"Hmmm." He took a deep breath and dropped into his chair. It squealed beneath his hefty frame. "Well, I'll tell you what. I'll give you until the end of the month."

"Really? Oh, thank you so much. You won't be sorry."

"I'd suggest you spend the time looking for a new job," he continued with a shrug. "I hear they're hiring receptionists down on the first floor. Now that's something a nice girl like you could handle. And you're bilingual. That's a plus." He smiled warmly, as if her entire future could be summed up in one such simple statement.

Her hands shook as she fought to regain her composure. "You don't understand, Mr. Nigel. My father brought our family to this country when I was just three years old. Back in Ensenada, life was hard. It was even harder once we got to L.A., but we made it. My dad took our little family business and turned it into something he's very proud of. We're all proud of him."

"Your point is?" He glanced at his watch.

"He took what little he had and turned it into much."

"And?"

"Don't you see?" she said. "I might be small. I might even be sweet, but I am supposed to be a reporter. I plan to take the little and turn it into much. Not for notoriety or anything like that. I just want to make a difference in this world."

"You and hundreds of other wanna-be's. What makes you so unique?"

His eyes bored into her. Angel stared back. "What sets me apart is my zeal, my drive. Nothing has ever come easily for me, but I've always been determined to succeed as a journalist. My professors at UCLA laughed when I told them I would one day work for KRLA. My own mother begged me to reconsider when the job offer came in. Everyone seems convinced I can't handle this job."

Mr. Nigel chuckled. "Shouldn't that tell you something? Be honest with yourself." He took a big swig from his coffee cup then leaned back in his chair with an exaggerated stretch. His rounded belly jiggled as he settled into place.

"Honesty is the best policy. At least, that's what I always say."

His comments carried some truth, and they stung. She didn't respond for a moment. When she did, her words were carefully thought out. "It's *honesty* that concerns me. And I need to be honest with you right now. You see, sir, I'm a kindhearted person. Always have been. I can't deny it. Maybe that's why I haven't found the perfect story to cover yet. They're all so, so—"

"Real?" He folded his arms.

She shook her head. "I was going to say 'depressing,' but if you insist."

He seemed intrigued at her sudden burst of energy. "Go on. I'm listening."

"I'd like to think that deep inside each one of us there is a bit of kindness, goodness. It's that side of reporting I'd like to explore. Those are the stories I'd like to tell. After all, not every news report has to have a negative twist. There are plenty of good stories out there waiting to be told. Happy stories."

Mr. Nigel shuffled the papers around on his desk in search of something. "Angel, you don't get it." Finally, he found a container of breath mints and snapped it open. As he popped one in his mouth, he added, "Happy stories don't elevate ratings."

"But they do elevate the spirit," she responded with a smile. "Maybe that's what I could do for KRLA." An idea came to her suddenly, one that could not be ignored.

"Elevate the spirit? Explain." His coffee cup nearly toppled off the desk as he set it down.

"Don't you see, Mr. Nigel? Maybe that's why I was sent here." Angel's excitement grew by the moment.

"*Sent* here? You mean, like from—" He pointed upwards.

She nodded. "Yes. I could be the reporter with a difference, the soft one. The one who looks for the good and finds it. I could be the—"

He finished the sentence for her. "The Voice of the Angels." His eyes filled with an excitement she had not seen before.

"Um, well, that wasn't exactly what I planned to say, but if that's what you think."

"It could work. It could work." His furrowed brow relaxed a bit. "You could be the good one. The kind one. The angelic one."

"Uh, right."

"The one who makes a difference."

She felt the corners of her mouth turn up as she spoke with confidence. "I would like to try, anyway."

"Okay, Angel, give me a night to sleep on this, and I'll give you my decision in the morning. In the meantime, be thinking of a slant, an angle—something to draw people in." His eyes narrowed as he seemed to disappear into his own private thought world.

"Really?"

"Really. Now get out of here. I've got work to do, and all that goodness is starting to rub off. I don't think I can handle much more."

"Of course, Mr. Nigel. Anything you say."

Angel left the office, trembling with relief and anticipation. She couldn't be sure, but she thought she heard him whisper the words "angelic visitation" as she went.

A whispered prayer crossed her lips. *God, I know there's got to be more to this reporting thing than tearing people down. I've seen so much of that, and I want to be a part of changing it. You didn't put me in this place by accident; I just know it. And You haven't placed me in the Los Angeles area by coincidence. I want to do some good in this city. I know I can, with Your help.*

With a renewed sense of purpose, Angel made her way back up to the fourth floor of the KRLA office complex, overwhelmed at the prospect of what the future might hold.

ॐ

Peter Campbell looked down at the dark-haired receptionist, who appeared to be preoccupied with painting her fingernails a shade of fire-engine red. The Costa Mesa sunshine streamed in through the window, causing the bold color to practically jump off her nails. The young woman smacked her gum as she worked, ignoring the ringing phone to her right. Her radio blared out a familiar love song. She sang along. Off-key.

Peter cleared his throat to get her attention. She remained fixed on the job at hand. When he did finally say something, determination laced his words. "Excuse me. I need to speak to someone about the Dumpster in your back parking lot."

She looked up at him, clearly frustrated at the interruption. Her expression changed dramatically when their eyes met. "Oooh. You're a cutie." She reached to snap off the radio.

"Um, thank you. But I really need to—"

"Great hair." Her bright blue eyes sparkled with excitement. "Who does your color?"

"My color?"

"Who highlights your hair? I just love all those different shades of blond. Must've taken hours."

As she stood to have a closer look, Peter forced his attention away from her plunging neckline. Her perfume nearly choked him. He flinched and took a step backwards as her fingers reached for a lock of his hair.

"Just washed out from the sun, I guess," he said. "Too many years out at Huntington Beach."

"Oh, you're a surfer." Her eyebrows elevated mischievously.

"Used to be."

"Well, you've certainly got the tan to prove it." She gave a little whistle. Peter felt his cheeks turn warm. "And look at those muscles," she added, giving his upper arm a squeeze. "Do you work out?"

"Uh, not really." He pulled away. "Lately I've been busy working. And that's what brings me here today."

"So, surfer boy, I've been thinking about highlighting my hair. What do you think? Should I go with reds or yellows?"

"I, um, I don't really know."

"I've been thinking about going platinum, but everyone tells me I'd look really great as a redhead."

Peter glanced at his watch, and she apparently took the hint. "Okay, okay. Enough about me. What was your question again?"

"Not really a question. I just need to speak to someone about the Dumpster in your back parking lot." *Someone who could pay attention would be nice.*

"Our Dumpster? What about it?"

He pointed to the logo on his shirt as he tried to explain. "I work for the city, the Sanitation Department. Recently we've noticed someone has been using your Dumpster to dispose of illegal substances."

"Oooh. Illegal substances. Sounds intriguing." She feigned a serious expression. "Tell me more."

Good grief. "I've noticed the presence of toxic substances during the last few pickups. A paint-stripping product. Someone in the building must be remodeling or something. But they can't leave products like that in the Dumpster. It's against the law."

"Uh-huh. I see." She clearly *didn't* see. Or care.

He forged ahead, undeterred. "The substances I'm referring to are hazardous. We recently handled a similar case on the other side of town. Over a dozen seagulls died after ingesting paint stripper residue found in a Dumpster outside a business complex. The management company was fined a pretty hefty amount once the EPA found out."

"So, you're one of those crazy environmentalists?"

"Well, not exactly."

"A bird-lover then?"

"I work for the city, ma'am. I collect and haul trash."

She shrugged. "Everyone's got to do something, I guess." She popped her gum and reached to snap the radio back on.

Peter took a deep breath and plowed into his carefully prepared speech. "The city has published new guidelines concerning the disposal of toxic substances, and your building manager needs to take a look at them."

She batted her eyelashes. "Wow. You do take your work seriously. What can I do to help, surfer boy?"

"I'm really only authorized to talk to the building manager, a Mr. Jake Whitestone. Do you know where I could find him?"

"Sure. I know where he is." Their eyes locked in a showdown of sorts.

"And that would be?" Peter tried not to lose patience.

"Last door on the right, Cutie. Suite 103. Tell him Darla sent you."

Finally. "Thanks." He turned to walk in the direction she had indicated.

Her voice trailed behind him. "Don't forget to stop back by on your way out. Maybe we can talk about something a little more interesting."

Peter shrugged and forced his attention to the matter at hand. He did take his job seriously. Always had. In the eighteen months he had worked for the city, he had fought to prove his worth, both to his family and friends. *I am making a difference in the world, even if I'm just a trash collector.* His occupational goals had never been lofty, though he knew his heart for the lost would make any job enjoyable and challenging. At least, as a sanitation worker, he found himself among those who were content to mingle with the ordinary people.

Unlike his father.

The elder Peter Campbell ran a well-known talent agency on Avenue of the Stars in L.A. His success as a businessman had afforded the family a beautiful home in Newport Beach. Nothing wrong with that. But the affluent lifestyle never sat well with Peter Junior. Expensive business dinners. Expense accounts. Lobster and caviar. He found himself more content working among the down-and-out. Inner-city ministries had become his passion. His greatest joy came from hours of volunteer work at the local feeding center for the homeless. Getting his hands dirty came naturally, which was why working as a trash collector made perfect sense.

At least to himself, if no one else.

Peter smiled, content in the fact that the Lord remained in control. Ironically, the Almighty appeared to have an amazing sense of humor as well. He had led Peter to the Sanitation Department, of all places. Dirty, smelly work— but he loved it.

He reflected on his current situation. Perhaps the Lord had more "cleaning" in mind than Peter had anticipated. *After that amazing sermon last Sunday, I know what God is asking of me. I've got to lay down this foolish family pride and be willing to humble myself. I choose to be different from the other men in my family. It's going to stop with this generation. Besides, it's not what I do that matters, it's who I am, and I know who I am in You, Lord.*

Peter did have a renewed sense of who he was, who he had become. And right now he was a crusader on a mission.

two

Angel tied the blue checked scarf around her hair, doing all she could to make herself look frumpy. She took one last look at her reflection in the small makeup mirror then tossed it into her purse before turning to show off her ensemble. "This isn't exactly what I had in mind."

Mr. Nigel beamed and nodded his approval. "You look like a million bucks, kid." He folded his arms with pride, as if he had accomplished some great feat.

"In this getup?" Angel had deliberately donned a worn pair of pants and a stained T-shirt with a tear on the sleeve. She had never felt more uncomfortable or more out of place.

"Yep."

She caught a glimpse of her reflection in the window and turned to analyze herself once more. "Do I look the part?" If she had to play a role, she wanted to play it right, all the way down to her toes.

"I guess." He shrugged. "Isn't that what the cleaning women in our building wear?"

"Yeah. Pretty close, anyway. All I need is a bucket with some cleaning supplies, and I'm in business. Where did you say I'm going again?" She pulled out her Palm Pilot, ready to jot down directions.

"Tennyson Towers in Costa Mesa. It's on Harbor, about three blocks up from the fairground. Fourteen hundred block. You'll be on the third floor."

"Mmm-hmm." She entered the information. "How long do you think this will take?" she asked. "Not that I mind this getup, but if we're talking long-term here—"

"That, my dear, is up to you. We'll see what kind of reporter you turn out to be. This gig should really help you develop your investigative skills. And not everyone has the opportunity to go incognito their first time out."

"I'm just so happy you're giving me this chance, sir." She smiled in his direction, hoping she exuded confidence.

"You wanted to work on a story that benefits people, right?" He seemed to come to life as he asked the question.

Angel nodded. "Of course."

"This will be a great start for you. These guys are skilled con men, telephone solicitors who've set up shop in a busy office complex. They're posing as an advertising firm, but our sources tell us they're probably not selling anything but a pack of lies. From what I can gather, they've been targeting the elderly, talking them out of thousands of dollars. Identity theft."

"Wow." She took a deep breath. "I've heard about that."

"They've been scamming people out of everything—from their social security numbers to credit card information. Then they create a huge mess, making purchases in other people's names. One of the elderly women who spoke to me—" He glanced at his computer screen. "A Mrs. Davidson— has been completely wiped out."

Angel realized for the first time the gravity of the job ahead. She really could make a difference in someone's life if she handled this story correctly.

"Living in a shelter right now because they robbed her blind. She's lost everything."

"No way. Isn't there something we can do to help her?"

"The station's working on that. But in the meantime, you get out there and get to work. And if you ever need any motivation, just think of an eighty-three-year-old great-grandmother named Ida Davidson who needs your assistance. She's counting on you, Angel. They all are."

He smiled in her direction, and she nodded a firm response. She would finally have a chance to do something wonderful—to help those who couldn't help themselves.

"This is serious business, and your work could be dangerous." Angel's stomach twisted in a knot as he spoke. "But if your story can put a stop to their dirty deeds—"

"Not if. When." She took a deep breath and lifted her chin. "And I'm not scared, sir. I'm really not."

He nodded. "When you stop them, you will gain the confidence of KRLA's elderly viewers and their families."

Angel sighed as she thought about those who had been hurt by these awful men. Who would defend them if she didn't? "I'm not doing this to gain popularity, Mr. Nigel. It breaks my heart to think good people are suffering. It really does."

His eyes twinkled. "Make sure you say that when the cameras are rolling. 'KRLA's heart is breaking for L.A.'s elderly victims.' "

"KRLA's heart?"

"Sure. But, Angel, you're not just representing KRLA. You're the voice of the innocents, the voice of—"

"The angels." His eyes lit up with renewed excitement.

She contemplated the daunting label—it was not one she felt terribly confident about.

"Now's the time, Angel." He opened the door, pointing her toward her future.

She nodded quietly, taking one last look at the large round

clocks on his wall. *10:15 a.m. in Los Angeles. 1:15 p.m. in New York. 6:15 p.m. in London. 7:15 p.m. in Paris. Just think, if I lived in Paris, this whole thing would be over with by now.*

Angel smiled at her boss and gave him the thumbs-up signal as she walked through the door. She struggled with her emotions as she made her way out to the parking lot. Moments later she pulled her silver sports car onto Interstate 405, deep in thought. A muttered prayer crossed her lips. "Give me courage, Lord. And protect me. These guys could be dangerous. They could be. . ." She stopped midsentence. No point in worrying about what they might be.

She glanced in the rearview mirror and contemplated her reflection once again. She had deliberately avoided makeup, opting for a natural look. Her olive skin glowed in the late morning sunlight, a sure sign the heat had gotten to her. She wiped away a bit of perspiration from her upper lip, noticing how small her mouth looked without the usual lipstick and liner. She felt genuinely uncomfortable without makeup, but it would have betrayed her.

Still, her reflection gave away too much. She looked far too. . .clean. That's what it was. Clean.

If I want to look like I've been working, I'd better add a few smudges to this clean face. And my nails. . . She looked down at her carefully manicured fingertips, nearly shifting lanes in the process. What should she do about her nails? Wear gloves? No, that wouldn't work. With a sigh, she began to scratch off the polish. As Angel traveled south, she chipped off layers of rose-colored polish, leaving her nails ragged and worn looking. *Mama would be horrified.*

By the time she arrived in Costa Mesa, she felt confident she could play the role required of her. She made her way down Harbor in search of the building in question. *Tennyson Towers.* Upon arriving, she peered up, her gaze coming to rest on the fourth-floor windows. "Okay. I can do this." She swallowed hard.

Angel inched her way into the parking lot then took one last look at her image in the rearview mirror. *Help me, Lord.* She conjured a mental picture of eighty-three-year-old Ida and forged ahead.

Mr. Nigel's words urged her on: *"She's counting on you, Angel. They all are."*

Her heart pounded unmercifully, and her hands refused to still themselves. Nevertheless, she made her way into the building and up to the fourth floor. There, standing before the oversized wooden door of Anderson Advertising Firm, Angel almost turned back, almost gave in to fear.

Then she thought of Ida once again.

She rapped on the door, but no one answered. "Hello?" She pushed the door open slightly, and her gaze rested on a man who sat behind a large, messy desk. He wore an "Angels" T-shirt. *Just a coincidence. Don't let it throw you.*

He glanced her way. "Can I help you?"

She noticed the nameplate on his desk: Jim Cochran. "I'm just here to clean, Mr. Cochran." She tried to hide the tremor in her voice.

"In the middle of the day? Don't you usually come in the evening?"

"Sorry." She shrugged. "This is my first day, actually. They didn't tell me when to come, just to come. Hope that's not a problem." She stepped boldly into the room, and he stood immediately.

"Well, I, uh." He glanced at his watch. "Tell you what, I'm

breaking for lunch in an hour. Can you come back then?"

"Sure, sure." She backed out of the room and closed the door.

An hour. What would she do for an hour? Angel lifted the heavy bucket and made her way to the ladies' room. She prayed she wouldn't run into anyone who might pose questions she couldn't answer. Strange—to think that she had to disguise her true identity in order to catch identity thieves. Ironic, really.

A woman in a navy jacket stopped her on the way in the door. "These bathrooms need a good cleaning. They're absolutely shameful."

Great. "I'll get right on it." *Why not? Might as well accomplish something while I'm waiting. It's not like I ever have to clean anything at home. The maids keep everything so nice.* Her mind drifted to the family's posh home in Bel-Air West, just off Mulholland. It was a beautiful Spanish Colonial home with rich woods and heavy draperies. A sweeping stairway curved from the bottom to the top of the foyer, beckoning visitors to enter. Angel had loved the home since childhood, though she had never stopped to consider all the sacrifices her father had made to offer her such a lifestyle.

Until now. From the day the family restaurant had taken off, her father had prided himself on making sure their every need was met. If he had any idea she stood here dressed like this, he would. . .

No point wondering what he might think. He'd just worry, anyway. Angel busied herself by spraying down the countertops and wiping them off. She looked inside the stalls, instantly growing queasy. "Yuck." She pulled out a bottle of cleaner and toilet brush and began the arduous task of cleaning the bowls as best she could. She worked up a sweat and reached with the back of her hand to brush her loose, damp bangs out of her eyes. *This cleaning stuff is no piece of cake.*

Angel glanced at her watch, shocked to find that an hour had passed—and then some. She shot a glance in the mirror as she tore out of the room. "Well, I really look the part now," she mumbled.

She made her way back to Anderson's, growing more nervous with each moment. Once inside, she would check the trash cans for evidence, something to support the claims these guys were ripping people off.

Angel tapped on the door again. No answer. *I hope they didn't lock up.* Nope. The door opened with no trouble. She eased her way inside. "Hello?" No response. "Anyone here? I've come to clean."

Total silence. She made her way across the room, pulled out a dust rag, and wiped down the desks and bookshelves as she went. "Better make it look like I've been here." Angelina pulled out a trash bag and emptied the can in the outer office into it. Tiptoeing, she made her way into the inner office. Her stomach churned with a mixture of excitement and fear. She glanced down at the desk, her gaze falling on a notepad. "Savelle. Close the deal tomorrow at two." She made a mental note and went about the business of dusting the desk. As she reached for the trash can, she heard a noise. Her heart jumped. "Hello?"

The man in the T-shirt appeared, worry lines framing his forehead. "You still here?"

"Yes. I'm nearly done." For the first time, she contemplated how casual his attire seemed for such a formal office. Too casual. *Suspiciously casual.*

He made his way into the office, his piercing gaze haunting

her. Angelina fought to keep her composure. She quickly emptied the trashcan into the bag and scurried out of the office, adding a courageous, "I'll see you tomorrow."

He turned his attention to the notes on the desk.

Angelina left quickly, grateful she hadn't aroused suspicion. "What am I going to do with this junk?" She clutched the bag of trash in her hand. "I'll have to look through this, but where?"

She wound her way through the hallways until she reached the elevator. The doors opened, and she found herself face-to-face with a cleaning woman. *A real cleaning woman.* The woman pushed a large rolling contraption filled with mops, brooms, and various cleaning supplies. *So that's what it looks like.* Nerves completely on edge, she stepped inside.

The older woman's carefully arched eyebrows elevated as she stepped out. "You new?"

"Uh, yeah."

The woman stuck out her hand. "I'm Mabel."

"Mabel," Angelina echoed.

"What are you doing up here in the afternoon?" Mabel asked. "I thought I was the only one who ever came in during the day." The elevator door began to close, separating the two.

"Nice to meet you." Angel waved as the door closed and leaned back against the wall, overcome with relief. "That was a close one." When the elevator stopped at the first floor, she exited looking down the hall toward the back door. *If I can get to the Dumpster out back, I can get rid of this trash.*

She clutched the bag with trembling hand, looking right, then left, for a trash bin. Ah. There it was. Thank goodness. *I just need to get out of here, get back into my car before someone asks me what I'm up to.* Lost in her thoughts, Angelina tossed the bag and her cleaning supplies into the Dumpster.

Instantly, she realized what she'd done. "Oh, no. I forgot to look through it for evidence." Oh well. There probably wasn't anything important there anyway. *Next time I can. . . Wait a minute. What if I can't get into the building next time? What if they catch on and I never get this opportunity again? I have to get that bag back. Now. I owe it to Mr. Nigel. I owe it to the people of Los Angeles.*

I owe it to Ida.

She stared helplessly up at the large green Dumpster and contemplated how she might accomplish the deed.

There was only one way.

❧

Peter pulled the large trash truck onto Harbor. The brakes squealed madly. "Come on. Come on." He still struggled when it came to maneuvering corners, even after all this time. More than one curb had become his friend over the past several months.

Harbor Boulevard teemed with cars—filled with impatient drivers. A horn honked behind him. He tried to pick up speed, shifting into second gear. The annoyed driver pulled around him, honking all the way.

"Sorry." Peter shifted into third. Up ahead loomed the Tennyson office complex. In the back parking lot he'd find a large container to empty. The last stop of the day. He always dreaded this one because of the heavy influx of traffic and the narrow area surrounding the Dumpster.

But he refused to allow the problem to stress him out. Once he finished up here, he would head out to the beach for an afternoon in the sun with some friends from church.

Plenty of relaxation awaited him, which made this last pickup more tolerable. Peter couldn't wait to tell his friends about what happened at the feeding center last night. A young man he had been witnessing to for months had finally given his heart to the Lord. He could hardly contain his joy.

Peter pulled into the parking lot, nearly hitting a blue minivan as it backed out of a parking space. *Watch where you're going!* Regaining his composure, he rounded the corner to the back of the building. *Ah. There it is. This shouldn't be too difficult. If I can just get this thing lined up right.* His brakes squealed once more as he squared the vehicle with the receptacle.

Peter reached down for the lever to release the arms. They would do the lifting. Everything from this point on would be a breeze. He relaxed slightly, blocking out the roar of grinding metal. The trash bin started to rise. Just as it reached eye level, something caught his attention and froze him to his seat.

A girl. There's a girl in the Dumpster!

three

Angelina shouted and waved her arms. "Stop! Stop this thing!" She stretched her petite frame to see over the top edge of the Dumpster, but what she saw almost caused her to lose her grip entirely. A huge trash truck had taken hold of the Dumpster with its long metal arms. The young man behind the wheel seemed lost in his thoughts, not once looking up.

"Stop! Do you hear me?" She felt the Dumpster jolt as it lifted from the ground. Her heart raced until she felt it would slip out her throat. The huge metal receptacle lifted, lifted, lifted into the air, and then tilted. Angel found herself face-to-face with the man in the truck. She flung her arms like a madwoman as she cried out, "Please, God, don't let me die like this! Not like this."

As if on cue, the young trash collector suddenly shifted his gaze and looked directly at her. His expression also shifted— to one of sheer terror. Immediately the Dumpster stopped rising. It rocked back and forth, back and forth, as she clung tightly to the edge. For a moment her entire world swayed, but she managed to keep conscious.

"Get me out of this thing!" Angel gestured toward the ground. The Dumpster slowly inched its way downward until it settled with a grunt onto the pavement. Angel collapsed into the trash as the large arms released their hold with a jolt. Every part of her anatomy trembled. The garbage, which seemed to vibrate around her, released the worst imaginable odor. From outside she could hear a man yelling, but she could barely make out what he said. Her head began to spin as the trash closed in around her.

"Are you okay, miss?"

She heard him clearly now, but Angelina could barely lift her head or think of a proper response. She felt strangely lightheaded, faint. The frantic voice seemed to draw nearer as everything around her began to turn. He was shouting now—an anxious, piercing shout. "I'm so sorry. I had no idea you were in there."

She should answer him, but she couldn't seem to force the words as her world spun on an unfamiliar axis. "I—I'm here." She stared up into the light. Bright yellow-orange, framed in shades of dismal gray. Sunlight, perhaps. Hard to tell right now.

"Please say something. I need to know you're all right." The voice grew nearer, and the man's anxious face peered over the rim.

He has a kind face, a gentle face. He almost looks like. . .a beautiful blond angel. His blue eyes gazed into hers with more compassion than she had ever seen before, then everything grew fuzzy. The Dumpster swallowed her alive. The sunlight faded, and everything in Angelina's world went black.

❧

Peter lunged over the edge of the Dumpster and found himself waist deep in putrid trash. He brushed a soiled piece of paper away from his mouth and tried to ignore the bitter taste it left behind. He waded his way over to the dirty young woman who lay so still in the corner and reached to feel her pulse. "Thank God. You're still alive."

No response.

"Miss, can you hear me? Are you awake?" She didn't stir. He continued to talk to her, desperate to awaken her. Nothing. A frantic moment or two passed, and Peter nearly gave up. *I should call the paramedics. I've got to get to my cell phone.* He scrambled up out of the heap and reached for the top of the Dumpster. Just as he got a good grip for springing over the edge, he heard a stirring behind him.

"Wha—what happened?"

He turned, thrilled to see the young woman's hands thrashing about. "I almost, I mean, I. . ." He struggled to find the words to say as he waded back over to her again. "It's all my fault."

"What's your fault?" She tried to sit up but immediately fell back again.

"Ooh, careful now." He slipped his hand under her head and gently lifted her body. "I'm going to get you out of here." *She's absolutely beautiful.*

"Whe—where am I, again?" Her eyes fluttered open and then closed almost immediately.

"In a Dumpster behind a building on Harbor."

"A Dumpster?" Her eyes shot open immediately. A horrified look crossed her face but melted quickly into acceptance. "Oh yeah. I remember now. That explains the smell, anyway." She attempted to sit up once again.

"Careful now." He took hold of her hand and helped her to stand. Together they made their way to the edge of the Dumpster, where he cupped his hands and offered her a step up. He got a good look at her ragged clothes for the first time. *What in the world is she doing in here, anyway? Maybe she was looking for food. Maybe she's. . .* A revelation suddenly hit him. *Maybe she's homeless.*

The young woman slipped a foot into his waiting palms and pulled herself up. She clung to the top with a vengeance. "Oh! I need help."

Yes, you do. And I'm going to make sure you get it. Peter scrambled over the edge to the ground below to help her down. "There. You made it."

She dropped to a sitting position alongside the Dumpster and clutched her head in her hands.

"Are you all right?" He took a closer look. The young woman's olive skin glistened in the sunlight, and her long, dark hair, though tangled and dirty, still caught his eye. Her deep brown eyes seemed to speak to him. This girl, whoever she was, was a knockout. A mess, but a knockout.

She nodded and her gaze shifted downward. Suddenly she came to life, her eyes widened in fear. "Oh my goodness! I need to get back in there." She struggled to rise to her feet.

"What?" What could possibly be so important?

"I left something in the Dumpster," she explained. "Something really important. I need it. Now."

The young woman's frantic words convinced Peter he had been right in his assumption. She had been looking for food. He should have guessed it from looking at her thin frame. Compelled by her desperation, he flew into action. "What do you need? Can I get it for you?"

"Oh no. Please. You've done enough." She fought to regain her composure and brushed dirt from her hair. "Just give me a minute and I'll—" She tried to pull herself up again but toppled backwards instead.

Peter caught her with little effort. "Whoa! Easy now."

A crowd gathered. People appeared from every direction. Some pinched their noses and turned the opposite direction.

Others offered cell phones, car rides, 911 calls—anything and everything. What had started as a private embarrassment quickly turned into a public sideshow. He cringed as people hollered out their distasteful comments. Then Peter turned his attentions back to the girl.

"Please make them go away." She spoke in a hoarse whisper. "I don't want anyone to see me like this." Her head tilted against the Dumpster in defeat.

Peter certainly understood the embarrassment and pride of the homeless from his years of working at the feeding center in Costa Mesa. They struggled with so many issues, and their personal feelings could not be ignored or taken advantage of in any way.

With that in mind, this beautiful child of God needed to be treated with dignity and respect. He did his best to disperse the crowd, though one or two lingered to watch his next few moves. He would treat her like a lady, regardless of her circumstances.

The young homeless woman looked up at him with tear-filled eyes. "I'm not having a very good day."

He smiled and tried to think of something brilliant to say. Nothing came to him. *Lord, I know this is no accident. I've been praying that You would use me in this job, and now You have. Give me the words to say.*

Her stomach rumbled, as if on cue, and her cheeks turned crimson.

Here's my chance, Lord. Thank You. He knew just what to do. "I'll tell you what. This was my last pickup of the day. Why don't you come with me, and I'll take you to lunch."

"Oh no, I couldn't possibly." She looked stunned. "I've got to get back to work; I can't stop now." She stood on wobbly feet. He wrapped his arm around her small waist, and the smell of shampoo struck him immediately. Odd. She must have bathed recently, though she could certainly do with a little cleaning up now.

He guided her to a sidewalk a few feet away. "Just let me lift this load, and we'll be on our way." In spite of her very loud objections, he jumped into the cab of the trash truck and started to lift the Dumpster once again. This time he made the transfer with no complications, though the look on the young woman's face below nearly broke his heart in the process.

"There." He climbed back out. "Piece of cake." *Oops. Poor choice of wording, perhaps.* She shook her head, staring up at the trash truck. *I'd better get her out of here before she climbs up into the back of the truck. She looks pretty desperate.* "What's your name?"

"Angel." She mumbled the word, her gaze never leaving the truck.

"Great name."

"Thanks." She gripped her head with her hands and stared off into space.

His heart nearly broke for her. She seemed so lost, so desperate. "Do you need a doctor, Angel?"

"No. I'm sure I'll be fine. I just need a minute to think. Nothing is making much sense to me right now."

He didn't doubt that. Hunger could drive people to near madness. He'd seen it dozens of times. "Maybe you'll feel better after a good hot meal." He reached to squeeze her slender hand and noticed her chipped nails.

She quickly hid them. "I—I guess."

He shifted his gaze. "I think you could use a nice distraction from what's just happened, and I happen to know there's a great little coffee shop around the corner. After nearly killing you, the least I can do is buy your lunch." He gave her his most compassionate look. "I owe it to you."

"Oh, I—I couldn't," she stammered.

"Of course you could. Doesn't a nice bowl of soup sound good? Maybe a sandwich?"

"Uh-huh." She continued to stare upward.

"So you'll come?"

"Come?" Blank stare.

"Well, it's settled then. Hop on in, Angel. And, by the way, my name is Peter. Peter Campbell."

❧

Peter Campbell. He looks like a Peter Campbell. Angelina's mind reeled as she took a couple of minutes to absorb all that had happened. The handsome blond angel ushered her into the cab of the trash truck. She took her seat and fought against the putrid smell that surrounded her on every side. *This is by far the craziest thing that has ever happened to me. I should get out of here. I should. . .*

Should she get into her own car and drive as far away from this place as possible? No. Not yet, anyway. Her mouth filled with saliva, and she feared she might be sick. Angel leaned her head back against the seat. *I should sit right here and let this pass.*

"Feeling okay?" He climbed into the driver's seat and shifted the vehicle into reverse.

She fought the nausea with every fiber of her being. "Just a little woozy. I guess I got pretty shook up."

"No doubt," he said as he backed the vehicle up. "And I'm so sorry. I hope you can forgive me for nearly dumping you out. I had no idea anyone would be in there. I've been making these rounds for months now, and I can assure you that has never happened to me before." He shifted into first gear and pointed the truck in the direction of the street. "This is certainly a first—for me, anyway."

"I understand. Listen. About why I was in the Dumpster. There's something you should know."

"No. Please. Don't tell me." He waved his hand in her direction. "I never meant to pry. I'm just glad you're all right, that's all." He smiled warmly at her.

"But—"

"No," he said. "Please don't feel the need to say anything. Let's just have our lunch, and then I'll take you wherever you need to go. It's the least I can do. Agreed?" He looked at her with large blue eyes.

Great eyes.

"Agreed." The feeling of sickness passed, and she leaned back against the seat, lost in her thoughts. *Mr. Nigel's going to fire me when he hears I didn't get those papers. He's going to. . .* The internal dialogue shifted to include the handsome young man to her left. He had appeared from out of nowhere—an angel in his own right. A handsome angel, she had to admit, who wore a dull gray uniform with the words "City of Costa Mesa" stitched across his chest.

As they passed her car, Angel quickly came to her senses. *What did I do with my keys? Oh, please Lord—don't let them be in the Dumpster.* She fished around in her pockets, relieved to hear the familiar jingle. She leaned back against the seat with a loud sigh.

"Everything okay?" The blond angel looked her way.

"Mmm-hmm." She relaxed and tried to imagine what she would say to Mr. Nigel when she got the chance.

If she got the chance.

Her mind began to wander. If she lost the job at KRLA, there were plenty of other stations in town. Surely someone would hire her. She played out several scenarios in her mind, but none felt right.

Ida Davidson is counting on me. I can't let her down.

A lone tear trickled down her cheek. She quickly brushed it away, determined to keep trying. For Ida's sake. For the sake of the other victims. She wouldn't give up. She would go back to Anderson Advertising again tomorrow and give this story another shot. She would find the information to put a stop to the identity thieves, and all of Los Angeles would thank her.

In the meantime, she would rest right here until her headache subsided and the world grew a little less fuzzy. Angel's stomach grumbled loudly, and she shifted her gaze to her driver, to make sure he hadn't noticed. He whistled along with a familiar tune on the radio, his eyes fixed on the road. She relaxed once again. After a good meal, everything would be better again.

"Here we are." Peter pulled into the parking lot of Kelly's Coffee Shop and parked on the far side, away from other vehicles. "Need any help inside?"

"No. Thanks." Angelina stepped down from the truck and onto the pavement. She excused herself to go to the ladies' room right away. *I stink to high heaven, and I'm sure I look just awful.*

People stared as she passed them on her way. "Don't worry, folks. I won't bite," she muttered. Once inside the restroom, she glanced at her reflection in the discolored mirror and realized instantly what they had been staring at.

Streaks of multi-colored dirt covered her face and T-shirt. Her hair was matted, and she wished like crazy she had a hairbrush with her. Like most of her other possessions, it remained locked in her silver sports car in the parking lot of Tennyson Towers.

She used a paper towel and some hand soap to scrub her face, and then did what she could to brush the dirt from her clothes. She worked her fingers through her hair until it looked more presentable. *Now, if I could just do something about the way I smell.* She looked around for something, anything. "Aha." Under the counter she found a spray can of air freshener. "It's not exactly a designer fragrance, but it will do." She sprayed herself, not just once but twice—hoping to erase the odor. *Now, I have to get back out there and say something sensible to that very nice guy with great blue eyes. He deserves that, at the very least.*

Angel walked back out into the restaurant and tried to ignore the stares from those she passed. One woman pinched her nose and waved her hand in front of her face—a sure sign she had overdone the air freshener. *Oh well. Maybe it will wear off by the time I get to the table.*

"What would you like to order?" Peter Campbell's inquisitive eyes stared into hers as she sat down.

She tried not to stare back, opting to look at his thick blond curls instead. "Uh. . ."

"Have anything you like. Anything."

I didn't have any breakfast, but I don't want to make a pig of myself in front of this guy. On the other hand. . . Her gaze fell on the colorful picture of a club sandwich with fries and a soft drink. *That sounds awfully good. And a bowl of soup would be nice, too.* She glanced at a picture of apple pie with ice cream on top, and her stomach grumbled loudly. *I hope he doesn't mind if I order dessert. I'm really famished.*

He sneezed suddenly and rubbed his nose.

She returned her gaze to the menu. "God bless you."

"Thank you." He sneezed again. "I don't know what's wrong with me. I really don't." He sneezed once more and reached for a napkin.

She winced. *I know what's wrong with you. It's this crazy air freshener. You're probably allergic. I know I am.* Her eyes watered unmercifully, and she dabbed at them with her napkin.

"Please don't cry, Angel. I know this whole situation is awful, but everything's going to be okay." He looked at her compassionately, and she felt as if her heart would melt.

"I'm not crying. I'm really not." She reached up to wipe her eyes. "I am ready to order now, though."

Peter gestured for the waitress. An older woman with a broad smile approached the table. She rubbed at her nose as she scribbled down their order. "Okay, that's a chef salad for you, handsome, and for the lady a club sandwich, extra tomatoes and bacon, with a double order of fries, a bowl of vegetable soup, and a large peach tea. Follow that with a slice of apple pie à la mode. Is that everything?"

"Yes. Whatever the lady wants."

Angelina looked up sheepishly into Peter's kind eyes. *I'm starting to think this guy's just too good to be true.*

four

"Tell me about this girl you've met, son."

Peter looked up from his breakfast cereal into his mother's teasing eyes. "How did you know I met a girl, Mom?"

Donita Campbell rinsed out the coffeepot as she responded. "I'm just guessing based on your level of distraction since last night. You hardly said a word during dinner; your mind seemed a thousand miles away. You're usually more talkative."

"Ah, true." Last night's dinner had been a fiasco of sorts. Peter had spent the entire meal lost in another world, one that revolved around an olive-skinned angel who had smelled anything but angelic. He couldn't help but smile as he remembered those sparkling eyes and tear-stained cheeks. What she had lacked in style, she had certainly more than made up for in personality and charm.

"Am I good, or what?" Donita raised her hands triumphantly. Her broad smile engaged him, as always.

Peter chuckled. His mother had a way of getting to the heart of a matter, even when he didn't feel like opening up. "You know me pretty well. But there's not that much to tell this time. Honestly."

She put on her best pouting face. "You always say that. But you can confide in me, honey. I just love a little romance, that's all." She winked at him in her usual cheerful way.

Who could blame her for craving romance, even if it was

37

not her own? Perhaps these conversations filled some void in her. His father, after all, wasn't much of a romantic.

"Come on now," she encouraged.

"Not much to share," he repeated. "I hardly know her; just met her yesterday, actually."

His mother filled the pot with purified water and reached for a bag of gourmet coffee. "Really? Where did you two meet? At the beach?"

"No. Not this time." Peter swallowed another mouthful of the sweet cereal and followed it with a gulp of orange juice.

"Church? I noticed there are a lot of new girls in the college and career class this semester."

"Nope." He wiped his mouth with an embroidered cloth napkin. *Should I tell her?*

She bit her lip. "At work, then?"

"Sort of."

"She works for the city?" A brief look of concern crossed her face before she turned her attention back to the bag of coffee.

"Not exactly." If his mother thought working for the city was a problem, just wait till she heard how Angel really spent her days. For a moment Peter contemplated opening up and telling his mom everything—his hopes, his suspicions, his fears. He could tell her he had prayed for a situation such as this, where he could reach out with his faith and help someone in need, someone who couldn't help herself. She would understand. She was, after all, the one who had encouraged him to follow his dreams.

On the other hand, if he shared anything about Angel, his mother would surely try to make something romantic out of it. Not only would she be off base, she would probably refuse to let go of the idea.

She drummed her fingertips on the countertop, finally snagging his attention. "Well, what does she do?"

"Hmm. I really don't know, Mom. I met her over at Tennyson Towers, but I don't think she works there." *Obviously.*

"What makes you think that?"

"I could just sort of tell. She wasn't dressed like an office worker or anything. To be honest, I don't know much about her."

His mother paused a moment as she popped open the bag of coffee. The aroma of hazelnut filled the room. "So, what's this mystery girl's name?" she asked as she measured out the dark brown crystals.

"Angel." He shifted his attention back to the cereal bowl and scooped out the last tiny raisin.

"Angel. Interesting." She grew silent and switched on the fancy coffeemaker. "You met an angel yesterday." He couldn't help but notice her grin.

"Looks like it." An angel in more ways than one, he had to admit. This girl had exuded a sweetness most people her age simply didn't possess, not even the girls at church. It had endeared her to him, though he couldn't be sure why. For some reason he felt drawn to her and very comfortable in her presence, despite their differences.

Peter's comfort around the homeless confirmed his desire to minister to their needs. He wouldn't allow intimidation or fear to stop him.

Or his father's biting comments.

The sizzle of hot water began almost immediately. His mother reached for an ivory porcelain cup. "Maybe she lives in the area," she suggested. "Just happened to be there visiting a friend or something."

"Or something." Peter tried to think of something to say to shift the conversation in a different direction. "Speaking of friends, how's Madeline?" His mother's best friend had just returned from a cruise to the Cayman Islands.

"Oh, she's great. Had a wonderful time. But she's got an awful sunburn. Red as a lobster. Just awful."

He smiled, thankful for the distraction. "That's awful."

"*You're* awful," she echoed. "And don't think I haven't figured out what you're up to. You're avoiding the subject."

"Maybe." He stared out the large French doors. The April sunshine reflected off the large swimming pool and caused a blinding glare.

His mother's face lit up suddenly. "I have a great idea, Peter. Why don't you invite your Angel over for dinner? Your father's entertaining a client tomorrow night, and that always bores me to tears."

How do I get out of this without hurting her feelings, Lord?

"I'd be happy to set an extra place at the table. What do you think?"

"I don't know, Mom." Tomorrow's dinner was sure to be spectacular, but Angel would stick out like a sore thumb. Surely she wouldn't have a decent thing to wear—not that Peter cared, but his father would. And if her performance in the restaurant yesterday was any indication, her table manners left something to be desired. Not to mention her smell.

Why am I even thinking about this? The whole thing is crazy.

His mother rambled on about the menu and then shifted the conversation to the table arrangement. Within minutes, she had the whole thing settled. "So, you'll ask her then?"

"I don't know, Mom. I'll really have to think about this."

"What's to think about? Be spontaneous! That's the boy

I know. Besides, it would be a great way to get to know her, right?"

Peter shrugged. "I guess." Not that she would ever, in a million years, agree to come. On the other hand, how would he ever know unless he asked her?

"Tell you what. I'll tell Gavin to prepare for an extra person, just in case. If it doesn't work out, that's fine." She dove into a discussion about the menu. "I'm thinking of serving that crab dip you love as an appetizer. Sound good?"

"Mmm-hmm."

"And for the main course, I think I'll go with salmon this time. And fresh steamed vegetables." She went on to discuss the merits of seafood.

Peter tried on several occasions to interrupt his mother, but to no avail. Like it or not, it looked like he had a date with an angel for dinner tomorrow night.

If he could ever find her again.

&

Angelina sat at the skirted dressing table in her bedroom and applied a thin layer of coral lip gloss. She gazed at her reflection one last time before standing. Yesterday's escapades had left her with a couple of bumps and bruises. Her left arm ached just below the elbow, and her right cheek was tender. She dabbed on an adequate amount of makeup to cover a blue spot under her right eye. No point in worrying her parents.

Or herself.

As she rose to her feet, she caught a glimpse of the Spanish four-poster bed in the mirror and smiled. *I love this room. I love the way I feel when I'm here.* Everything about this place spoke of safety, security. *If I could just stay here forever. . .*

But that would defeat the purpose. Besides, she had spent enough time locked in fear. The Lord had already set her free from that cage. Wonderful possibilities awaited—if only she could maintain the courage to put one foot in front of the other each day.

Angel made her way to the edge of the bed and pulled on a pair of worn tennis shoes. She sighed as she looked down at the ragged clothes she had selected for today's adventure—a rumpled T-shirt and black stretch pants. They looked dingy against the stark white eyelet comforter folded at the foot of the bed.

Her mother tapped on the open door and stared at her with curiosity. "Going to the gym?"

"It's for my job, Mama. I'm going undercover." *Better leave it at that.*

"Undercover? You mean you're working on an assignment?" Her mother's thinly plucked eyebrows elevated. "They've given you a story?"

"Yes. A really big story." Angel gave her a reassuring smile.

"So tell me all about it."

"I'm sorry, Mama. I can't give away any information. I just can't."

Her mother looked stunned. "Even to me—your own mother?"

"Even to you," she explained. "It's company policy. When I work undercover, it's like being on a secret mission. When the story breaks, you'll know everything, I promise."

Her mother began to fuss with the comforter, patting out a couple of wrinkles. "I see."

"Mama. . ." *She doesn't see, but she's too gracious to say so.*

"Nothing too dangerous, I hope. Your father and I were

worried when you came in last night. You looked, well—"

"I know. I looked awful." Angel hoped to reassure her precious mother. *Lord, don't let her worry too much. Let her know You're taking care of me.*

Her nose wrinkled. "Smelled awful, too, if you don't mind my saying so."

"Thanks."

Her mother's face grew serious. "We're really proud of you, Angel, but we're a little worried, too. Especially your papa. He wants to protect his little girl."

"But that's just it," Angel argued. "I'm not a little girl anymore."

"I know, I know. You're twenty-two, Angelina." Consuela Fuentes spoke the words fervently.

Angel sighed. *I know what's coming.*

Her mother picked up the hairbrush from the table and pulled it in long strokes through her hair. "Twenty-two."

Angel relaxed as the brush made its way through her thick hair. "What are you saying, Mama?"

"I married your father at nineteen. By the time I reached twenty-two, I had already been married three years. Your brother was potty-trained, and you were cradled in my arms."

Here we go again. The story.

"I spent my days singing nursery rhymes in Spanish and pushing strollers to the market. That's what twenty-two looked like for me." She placed the brush on the dressing table.

"Things are different now, Mama. People are waiting to get married, even in our culture. They're establishing their careers first. That's what I want to do." She tried her best to sound firm, yet respectful.

Her mother shook her head. "Angel, Angel."

"Do you think I shouldn't work because I'm a woman? Is that it?" Angel stood to make up the bed. She pulled the crisp white sheets first, followed by the white eyelet comforter—a gift from her Aunt Ricarda in Ensenada, Mexico, just an hour south of the California border but light years away in all other respects.

"No, honey. I'm a firm believer in hard work. I worked for many years as a girl, and I'm not afraid of getting my hands dirty now, either. I'm just saying that security, real security, comes in relationship with God first, family second, and job third. You've got to have your priorities straight."

Angelina sighed. "I understand that. I really do. But before I can put family first, I have to find a husband."

"Exactly."

She groaned. "Mama, it's not so easy. Especially these days."

"Easier if you would keep your eyes open. You always stay so focused on your job you forget to watch for a husband. The Lord could drop one in your lap, and you might not see him."

"Mama."

"I want you to have a good job, if that's what you want. I know having a career is important to young women these days. I want that for you. But I also want you to know the joy of finding love. It makes all of the work more tolerable—gives you something to work for."

"I know." *I do want a husband and family someday. Have I really been so focused on my job that she thinks I'm not interested in marriage?*

"Your father has worked so hard to provide this beautiful home for us." Her mother smiled as she gestured around the room with its rich, imported furniture. "His work has always been for his family."

"I know." Years of work had earned Felipe Fuentes a prestigious family restaurant and a lovely home. None of these things were taken for granted. Ever.

Lord, we have so much to be grateful for. You've given us a whole new life, and we don't ever want to forget to thank You or remember where it all came from.

"There's a lot to be said for home and family." Her mother embraced her tightly. "Never forget that, Angel."

"I won't." She stepped back and looked down at her attire one more time. "Guess this is as good as it's going to get."

"No, honey." Her mother wagged her finger. "It's only going to get better from here. I feel sure of it."

Angel glanced at her watch and immediately sprang into action. "It's nearly ten o'clock, Mama. I'm going to be late." Excitedly, she raced for the door.

five

The tires on Angel's silver sports car squealed as she pulled into Tennyson Towers. Her heart raced as she glanced down at her watch. Noon. She whipped into a parking space on the side of the building and paused only long enough for a quick glance at her reflection in the mirror. She looked frumpy enough and felt confident about the job ahead, but what could she do about her lack of cleaning supplies?

Hopefully, there would be plenty of time to worry about that later. She bounded from the car, full of nervous energy. As she raced toward the building, she prayed the advertising office would be empty. If so, she would take the place by storm. She would find all the evidence she needed, and then some. She would take it to Mr. Nigel, and all would end well.

If her plan worked. Somewhere between L.A. and Costa Mesa, Angel had established a strategy of sorts. She would enter the office with no one else around. First she would look for copies of anything that seemed suspicious—social security cards, driver's licenses, or credit cards, in particular. Then, if she worked up the courage, she would attempt to access their computer.

Unless it was password protected, in which case she would have to think of something else. Once inside the computer she would look for database files. Anything with names and addresses. She would make some calls. She would locate some victims. Then she would figure out a way to involve the police.

Angel's stomach began to churn, just thinking about it.

She nodded at a man in a stiff black business suit as she made her way through the door and toward the elevator. The wheels in her head turned and anxious thoughts tumbled forth. She prayed she wouldn't run into Mabel because she didn't want to be deceptive.

She breathed a sigh of relief as she reached the fourth floor without incident. *Thank You, Lord.* She walked down the long, narrow hallway to the door of the so-called advertising firm, anxious to do some real scout-work. *Once I get inside, I'll go straight to the desk in the front office. I'll open every drawer. I'll check every bookshelf. Then I'll move to the back office. I'll check every corner of the room. And if I get caught without cleaning supplies in my hands, then I'll. . .*

Hmmm. . .

Angel forced herself to remain courageous. If they walked in on her, she would simply grab a trash bag from the nearest can and begin filling it. But first she had to make it inside. She rapped on the door lightly, her nerves on edge. She stood for some time, awaiting a response.

Nothing. She breathed a sigh of relief and thanked God they had already left for lunch. Much work lay ahead of her today. Today she would crack this case wide open. Today she would prove to Mr. Nigel that she had what it took to be a real reporter. Today. . . She reached for the door handle.

Locked.

She tried the knob again, refusing to give in. Nothing. "This can't be happening. I've got to get in there."

A woman in a fitted gray suit approached. She looked down her long, thin nose at Angelina. "Lose your keys?"

"No, I, uh—"

"What are you doing here in the middle of the day? Don't you people usually clean at night?"

You people? Angel swallowed her pride and fought for an answer. "I'm on a special assignment. This place is especially dirty."

The woman's face softened a little. "You're telling me. These guys are dirty, and I don't just mean their office."

"Really?" Angel's reporter antenna went up immediately. "What do you mean?"

The woman looked around to make sure no one was listening. "Call it a whim, a notion. Whatever. They just seem sleazy to me. That one guy—the one who always wears the T-shirts—he's been hitting on girls in the elevator. And that other one—the guy with all the tattoos—he's just plain creepy."

Angel took mental notes as the woman spoke.

"Neither one owns a suit. Very suspicious. I don't have a clue what they're up to, but if they're in the advertising business, I'll eat my hat."

Angel's excitement grew, though she tried not to let it show. *Stay cool, calm.* "I just need to get in there to clean."

"Would you like me to call the building manager?" The woman pulled out a cell phone and flipped it open. "They've always got extra keys. I lost mine just last week, and they bailed me out. Only took about five minutes."

Angel's heartbeat thudded. "That's not necessary. Really. I can just come back later."

The woman shrugged then pushed the phone back into her purse. "Just trying to help."

"Thanks," Angel called after her. The woman waved her hand and disappeared around the corner.

Angel collapsed against the wall. *Lord, this is too hard. I didn't think it was going to be like this.* Defeated, she turned back toward the elevators. She tried to think of a plan, tried to come up with another idea, but nothing came to her.

Moments later, she made her way out of the building. She looked up at a cloudy sky, lost in her thoughts. "What am I supposed to do now?" Her heart nearly broke as she thought about how she had failed. Again. Dejected, she reached into her pocket for her car keys.

Empty. "You've got to be kidding me." Had she lost them in the building? She didn't want to have to go back in there. Not today. She replayed the events of the last few minutes. No. She hadn't carried any keys into the building. She must have left them in the car.

Angel wound her way around the building to the side parking lot, where her silver car sat, glistening in the afternoon sun. She glanced through the driver's side window, amazed to find her keys dangling in the ignition. "Oh, no. Now what?"

She always carried a spare key in her purse, but the purse, unfortunately, remained in the car as well. A third key hung on the wall at home. Little good that would do her now. She leaned against the hood of the car, deep in thought. Immediately the car alarm went off.

Angel covered her ears and tried to think. "I can't call home anyway. I've got no cell phone. My whole life is locked up in this car." The alarm continued to ring out.

Instinctively, she began to pray. *Lord, if You'll get me out of this, I'll. . .* Well, no point in making rash promises. Angel wasn't sure what she would have promised, anyway. A shimmer to the right caught her eye, and she looked down into the grassy area that separated Tennyson Towers from the service station next door. "What's that?" She reached down and picked up a piece of wire.

❧

Peter ended his shift and climbed into his car to head home. If traffic didn't present much of a problem, he might have time to stop off at the feeding center on his way to double-check some supplies.

He squinted against the afternoon sunshine. He had so many things on his mind, including thoughts of Angel. His interests in her weren't romantic—not at all. He saw her as someone who needed his help. Problem was, he hadn't yet figured out a good way to pray about this situation. He fought to formulate the words.

Lord, I know You've led me to Angel. She's Your child, and You love her just as much as You love me. Thank You for giving me a chance to make up for the mistakes of the other men in my family. I'm going to do some good in this world. Help me accomplish that, Father. Let me start with this poor, lost girl.

Something inside told him to swing by Tennyson Towers on his way home. Perhaps, for lack of a better place, she had set up residence there. It had seemed that way when he dropped her off after yesterday's lunch anyway. Maybe he could find her and. . .

Peter wasn't sure what he'd do if he found Angel today. It would look like too much of a coincidence if he just happened by, wouldn't it? He struggled with what he would say, should she see him. He didn't want to be deceptive, but he did feel a need to help. She looked like someone who could use some serious help.

As he turned onto Harbor, Peter prayed. Tennyson Towers

beckoned from a distance. He slowly drove to the front of the building, where he hoped to catch a glimpse of Angel. Nothing. Pulling into the parking lot, he spied her. *There she is. What in the world?* She stood alongside a silver sports car with a metal coat hanger in her hand. She fought to get the car unlocked—or so it would seem.

Oh, Lord. Has it really come to this? Is she stealing, too? He contemplated the idea. *Should I do something? Should I say something?* He could hear the car's alarm now—blaring loudly. She seemed to ignore it as she worked feverishly to get the car open. Peter watched it all, horrified yet intrigued. None of this seemed to make sense, and yet he couldn't deny the reality of what he was seeing with his own eyes.

Angel reached up with the back of her hand to wipe the sweat from her brow, clearly unaware of his presence. He inched his car along, hoping not to arouse her suspicions. Just as he passed behind the silver vehicle, she dropped the piece of wire and stepped away from the car, hands up in the air.

As if waiting for a police car to come along.

He struggled with his emotions, trying to decide if he should telephone the police or just leave and pretend he had seen nothing. He opted to wait—at least a few minutes more. "I've got to give her another chance."

Just then she turned and walked toward the building. For a brief moment she looked his way. He turned his head quickly. She made her way toward the back of the building once again. Peter pulled into a parking space, prepared to wait as long as it took.

What he was waiting for, he couldn't be sure.

❧

"Hello, Nardo? Can you do me a favor?" Angel tried to hide

the quiver in her voice as she spoke over the borrowed phone to her older brother. The alarm shrieked in the background, making it nearly impossible to hear.

Or think.

"What's up, Angel?" He sounded agitated. She must have interrupted his work.

"I need someone to come and rescue me."

"Rescue you?" Now he sounded worried.

"Sort of. I locked my keys in my car." She bit her lip and waited for his predictable response.

He groaned. "Is that your alarm I hear?"

"Yeah."

"Angel. Not again. This is the third time in a month."

She wiped the perspiration out of her eyes. "Yeah. Only this time I'm a lot farther away."

He groaned again and asked the question she had been waiting to hear. "Where are you?"

"Costa Mesa. Tennyson Towers."

"You've got to be kidding me. When are you going to learn? I told you to get the car with the keyless entry. Remember, Angel?"

"Yes, I remember, but—"

"I know. I know. You thought it wouldn't be safe. You were worried someone else might break in. Now you're in a car that no one can break into. Even you."

"Nardo, please, watch your temper. And please come get me."

"I'm coming, Angel. But don't you dare say a thing about how I look."

"Meaning?"

"Meaning I'm in my workout clothes. I just got home from the gym. I look awful and smell worse."

"I don't care about that." She sighed. "Just come and get me, okay?"

"I'll be in Pop's old car. Mine's being painted, remember?"

"I remember. Just hurry, Nardo." Angel placed the phone down and thanked the receptionist in the law office before turning to leave. She shuffled toward the back of the building, where she dropped down onto a concrete bench. She fought with her own emotions, trying to figure out why nothing seemed to be going her way today. Tears tumbled freely. She couldn't seem to stop them.

For some reason, her thoughts immediately raced to one of her favorite Scripture verses in the book of James, one she had been studying diligently in preparation to teach a Bible study at church next month.

"Consider it pure joy, my brothers," she whispered to no one but herself, "whenever you face trials of many kinds, because you know that the testing of your faith develops perseverance. Perseverance must finish its work so that you may be mature and complete, not lacking anything."

Lord, I'm having a hard time finding any joy in the middle of this trial. I know that my faith is being tested. That's for sure. But I'm not sure I can persevere. Right now, Lord, I'm not sure I can take one more step.

Just as she brought her face to rest in her palms, the alarm, mercifully, went off.

❧

Peter watched from a distance as Angel buried her head in her hands. *Is she crying?* He argued with himself about whether to join her or leave her sitting there alone. If he approached her, what would he say? Would he summon the courage to present the gospel message?

Finally the decision was made. He would approach her, talk to her. He would take the time to listen, which would build a bridge of trust between them. Once trust had been firmly established, Angel would be happy to listen to what he had to say. Peter would then share the gospel, using all the tools he had been trained to use. She would respond. All would end well.

Or so he prayed.

He parked his car and prayed for God's favor as he made his way across the parking lot toward her. As he approached, he couldn't help but notice the tearstains on her cheeks and the red, swollen eyes. "Angel?"

She dabbed at her puffy eyelids. "Oh, no. Not you again."

"Peter. Peter Campbell."

"Right. I remember." She gazed at him for a moment and then shook her head.

Peter stood silently for what seemed like an eternity, hands gripped together. "What's wrong? Is there anything I can do to help you?" He sat and turned his full attention to her.

"No. I'm fine. Really." She sniffled and rubbed at her runny nose with the back of her hand.

"You're not fine. Something terrible has happened. You can tell me." He slipped his arm around her shoulder and prayed she wouldn't find him too forward.

Instead, she buried her head in his shoulder. "Did you ever have one of those days?" she asked, now sobbing.

"Of course. We all do."

"Well, I'm having one today." She sniffled. "Nothing is going right. Nothing."

Peter nodded, and his heart swelled with anticipation. *Thank You, Lord. She's really opening up.* "Isn't there something

I can do? Would you like to go someplace and talk?"

She shook her head. "No. Just please sit here with me awhile. I don't like to be by myself."

Ah. The truth came out at last. Angel's time on the street had apparently opened her eyes to the loneliness, the desperation. She clearly recognized the hopelessness of her situation, but how could he make things better? What could he say to help?

"I don't blame you," he said finally. "What would you like to talk about?"

She shrugged. "The weather. Anything. I don't care."

He began at once to discuss the possibility of rain. Angel smiled as he pretended to do the weather report with a British accent. She softened even more as he shifted to sports, and laughed aloud as he pretended to play the role of sportscaster.

Then the conversation turned a bit. They began to talk at length about a local ball player who had recently struggled with a drug problem. She seemed to be receptive to his attempts to interject God into the conversation, even adding tidbits of wisdom that amazed him.

They talked for ages. Funny, for someone who lived on the streets, she sounded educated. Really educated. The conversation shifted from their unrecognized dreams to the condition of the world. For more than an hour they talked. And talked.

Peter spoke frankly of his relationship with the Lord. He told Angel of God's love and faithfulness in his own life. He shared with her the dreams God had given him to better his life—to make something of his existence—and not to waste away with anger as his father had. He told her that God had placed a call on him to touch lives, to make a difference. She listened quietly and nodded as he spoke. As if she knew and understood.

Peter's heart soared. *Lord, she seems receptive.*

He looked up as he heard a horn honking. A rough-looking guy in a beat-up old car gestured for Angel to join him. *Surely she's not going to. . .*

She stood abruptly, her gaze traveling to the car. "I, uh, I have to go now. But thanks for the conversation."

Peter's heart pounded against his chest wall. "Angel, you don't have to go with that man. I could take you wherever you want to go. Really." He gave her his most imploring look, but she seemed unmoved.

The horn honked repeatedly, and the guy inside looked perturbed. *Who is that guy? What does he want with her?*

"No, I really have to go," she said softly. "Please don't worry about me. I'll be fine." She crossed the parking lot to the car, leaning in to take something from the man inside.

Despondent, Peter turned and walked the other way.

six

Peter spent a near-sleepless night worried about Angel's condition and wondering what he could do to help her. His prayers that God would send someone he could minister to had been answered. But now what? Her needs seemed so great. What could he, one lone person, do to help someone in such a hopeless position? All night long he tossed and turned as he tried to figure out how he should intervene on her behalf.

Or even *if* he should intervene on her behalf. Would it be appropriate for a man, even one fully committed to the Lord, to minister to a young woman he barely knew? Would he be breaking some sort of protocol by doing so? Should he ask for help from some of the girls from church? One of the girls from the singles' ministry perhaps? If so, who would he ask? Who could truly connect with Angel as he had?

He *had* connected with her, hadn't he? Peter's spirits lifted as the Lord reminded him of the connection just today. But why had she chosen to leave with that awful man? The question tormented him. He should have stopped her, should have intervened.

Through the sleepless hours, the Lord continually brought to mind the story of the Good Samaritan. The Samaritan hadn't turned his head and looked the other way when he came across someone others neglected. But neither had he taken a long-term, overcommitted interest. He had simply given the injured man a place to stay and provided for his immediate needs.

Perhaps that's all God required of Peter as well. He could, at the very least, provide for Angel's immediate needs and make sure she had a place to stay—a safe place where she wouldn't have to worry about digging through garbage to find food or scavenging through bathrooms to clean herself up. He drifted off to sleep, but fitful dreams haunted him till morning.

The sun rose and so did Peter, stiff and sore. He contemplated many things as he dressed for work. One thought simply would not leave his mind. His desire to help those in need seemed to be birthed out of a need in his own life. After years of carefree living, he had finally come to the conclusion that his life needed some direction, a sense of purpose. He had always been a believer, for as long as he could remember, but he had squandered so much time in his youth. And so much money. Recent sermons, coupled with personal promptings from the Holy Spirit, had shown him how far he had drifted from God's plan for his life. Could he make up for it now?

Yes, he reasoned as he made the drive to Costa Mesa—he would make up for lost time. Out of a sincere desire to be useful, Peter would help Angel and others like her. If he had ever doubted this call of God on his life, it was all crystal clear to him now. If Peter had his way, he would someday open a home for people in need.

Someday.

That dream did not arise from his meeting with Angel, but spending time with her had confirmed it. He would help those who could not help themselves. Something even beyond what the feeding center could afford to offer. He longed to open a transitional living center for those coming off the streets. They needed a recovery program and a place to be trained for jobs.

His ideas flowed freely. So did the questions. Where would he house people? Who would assist him? How could he even begin? Could he keep his current job to fund the plan, at least until the ministry could stand on its own feet? He examined his motivations and concluded that his heart remained pure before God in this matter. His heavenly Father would support him. Even if his earthly father refused.

For a second, Peter tried to envision the look on his father's face when he shared his dream with him. He would never understand, but then again his father never seemed to understand anything Peter said or did. They were two different men.

From two different planets, it seemed.

Peter struggled with a particular memory of his father, one that had always bothered him. When he was seven years old, his father, then a new agent, came home with a proposition one night. "One you won't be able to turn down," he had said with a forced grin. "It's a commercial for a young boy. Peanut butter. You're the kid they're looking for, Peter. I know it. Blond hair. Blue eyes. Full of life."

His dad had gone on to explain why it was so critical to fill this position quickly. He was trying to make a name for himself in the business. If he could just get this one account, it would open a host of other doors for him.

But Peter didn't want to do it. He had clung to his mother's skirts and cried. The thought of standing before those cameras terrified him. He wouldn't do it—not for his dad or anyone else. He just couldn't.

Peter even lied, telling his father he didn't like peanut butter. His father had bribed, cajoled, and finally threatened. In the end, he got his way, and his father lost the account. But he would never forget his father's words: "That's the last time I offer you anything."

And it pretty much had been. As he grew, the relationship with his father also grew—more distant with each passing day. Peter had always felt like such a disappointment, on so many levels. By the time he reached manhood, he and his father were two different men, going two different ways—his father following the path of money and fame, and Peter following the road of ministry. He had found his true identity in the Lord and knew that God would honor his choices.

But his father. . .

Well, no time to worry about that now. Peter had job obligations. And a lost sheep to tend. Not to mention great plans for the future. Somehow all of these things would come together into one glorious picture.

He spent the rest of his drive in deep prayer for his parents, his coworkers, and his friends at church. Finally, when he could resist thinking about Angel no longer, he prayed for her. His words flowed freely and loudly. At one point he noticed someone in another car staring at him. He focused on driving.

By the time Peter reached Costa Mesa, he found himself strengthened and fully awake. He took his place behind the wheel of the trash truck, a man with new resolve and clearer direction.

"Lord, if it's Your will for me to find Angel, please guide me to her." He prayed aloud once again as he made his way along the now-familiar route down Harbor Boulevard. Tennyson Towers loomed in the distance, beckoning him.

"If she's not there, I'll know I'm supposed to drop this. But if she is—" He stopped, not knowing quite what to say next.

He bit his lip, a habit from early childhood, as he turned into the parking lot. His gaze shifted this way and that as he searched for her. No Angel. He maneuvered the truck to the back parking lot. *Surely she won't go near the Dumpster again. Maybe she won't be here at all. Maybe she. . .* He let his mind wander as he looked in every conceivable direction. A sudden fear gripped him. *She's not here—and I'm never going to see her again.*

❧

Angel pulled into the back parking lot of Tennyson Towers and exited her car with great excitement. She opened her trunk and took out a large yellow bucket she had just purchased at a local superstore. Then she reached for her laptop, which she carefully wedged into the bottom of the bucket.

Next she reached for the bag of cleaning supplies, which she gingerly pressed in around the computer. Angel mentally crossed each one off her checklist as she went: a large bottle of ammonia, glass cleaner, furniture polish, four sponges, and a couple of large pink dust cloths. If things went as planned, she would never have to use any of these items.

Finally, on top of everything else, she placed a paper plate filled with gourmet chocolate chip cookies, wrapped in clear plastic wrap. These she would use for a diversion.

Heaving the bucket, she made her way toward the back of the building, where she hoped to make a smooth, quick entrance and head straight to the fourth floor.

All the way to Costa Mesa she had toyed with new ideas, ways to find the evidence she needed. Today's approach would be completely different from yesterday's, and having people in the office would help her case, not hurt it. The chocolate chip cookies would make a nice peace offering should the need arise.

She looked up as she heard a memorable sound. A massive trash truck loomed in front of her. The Dumpster rose slowly—a familiar sight. She strained to see the driver. *Oh, no. It's him. If I'm careful, maybe he won't see me. Maybe he won't. . .*

Peter beeped his horn. She waved and muttered to herself, "I'll just keep walking."

As the Dumpster hit the ground, the truck engine shut off, and the young man leaped from the driver's seat. "Hey there, I was hoping I'd run into you. How are you today?" His tan cheeks were slightly more flushed than she remembered, his words breathless.

She glanced at her watch. "Fine. Just in a hurry." *Lord, help me. I don't want to hurt his feelings, but if I don't get up there in the next few minutes, I'll be out of time.* Then again, why would she want to avoid those amazing blue eyes and shaggy blond hair? He had rescued her, after all. He was her very own personal angel. She owed him a few moments of conversation after what he had done for her.

"Oh, I'm sorry." Peter's smile faded a little. "I was hoping we could talk. I've been thinking about you a lot since yesterday. I've been a little worried about you." His gaze shifted to the ground, then his eyes riveted on hers once again.

She forgot all about the time. "You have?" Angel shifted the bucket to her other arm.

"Well, more concerned, really. I was wondering if we could get together for a cup of coffee. I'd like to talk." His gaze drifted to the yellow bucket with gourmet cookies perched on top.

"I—I don't know." Angel glanced at her watch. "I really need to go. Now."

"I just wanted to ask you something." He looked hurt.

She turned toward the building and took a few steps away from him. "I'm sorry. I've really got to go."

"How long do you think you'll be here?" She turned back. Those amazing eyes locked into hers once again.

If you keep looking at me like that, I'm never going to make it inside. "I'm not sure. Probably an hour. Maybe a little longer."

"What if I came back?" he said.

"Well, I guess, but I really—" She shrugged and pulled the door open.

"I know. You have to go now." He suddenly sprinted toward her. "Look, Angel, to be honest, I just wanted to invite you to a dinner at my house tonight. My parents are throwing this dinner party. I was hoping you would join us."

"I'd love to." *What am I saying?*

"Really? Well, in that case, I could pick you up around—"

"I won't need a ride. Just an address." She glanced nervously at the building and prayed the fourth-floor office would be open.

"Are you sure?"

"Yep."

He reached into his wallet and pulled out a business card. "The address is right here. The house is in Newport Beach. If you're sure."

"I'm sure. See you tonight." She turned abruptly, waving as she went. Angel entered the building and breathed a sigh of relief. *I need everything to go smoothly. Lord, please help me find something useful today—something that will help stop these guys in their tracks. And protect me, Father. Please.* The elevator door opened, and she caught her breath as Mabel stepped out.

"Well, hey there, honey," the older woman said. "Haven't seen you in a couple of days. Thought maybe I'd dreamed you up."

"Nope," Angel mumbled as she stepped onto the elevator. "I'm the real deal."

"You must be the new girl they told me about. I'm supposed to be training you."

"Oh." Angel's heart leaped to her throat. "I didn't know about that. I was just—"

"Glenda Miller, right? Funny, you don't look like a Glenda."

"Oh, well, that's because I—"

"I knew you were coming," Mabel interrupted, "but those folks up in management never give me specifics. "So, what do you think of the place, Glenda?"

"It's, uh, it's nice," Angel said as she shifted the large bucket from one arm to the other.

The elevator door started to close, but the older woman reached with a strong arm and wrestled it back open again.

"What did you do—bring your own stuff?" Mabel motioned to the large bucket.

"Yeah. Thought it would be a good idea."

"No need, hon. There's a closet in the basement full of supplies. I'll show you everything this evening when you come back."

"Oh, okay. Well, I'd better go. I was just headed up to the fourth floor."

"I don't think so, baby girl," Mabel said with a wink. "Management office is on the seventh floor. Good news is they've posted your hours. Just saw them myself. You don't really need to be here till 6:30."

An older man stepped on the elevator and impatiently pushed a button for the fifth floor.

"Oh, really?" Angel looked back and forth between the two of them.

"Yep. I'll be back to train you then. I just stopped by to pick up my check. I'll meet you down in the basement."

The man cleared his throat. Loudly.

"Oh, well, I . . ." Angel's heartbeat pounded in her ears. She could barely hear herself think.

The man gave her a glare that could not be ignored, and Mabel released her hold on the door. "Basement at 6:30," she called out.

The door shut, separating them at last. Angel dropped her bucket of cleaning supplies, and they spilled out. The expensive chocolate chip cookies went everywhere, but they were the least of her worries. The man turned his head, clearly not wanting to help.

My computer.

As the elevator went up then down, down then up, she worked feverishly, scooping up bits of cookie and colorful sponges. Thankfully, the computer appeared to be safe.

By the time she stepped out onto the fourth floor, Angel's nerves were shot. Determined to forge ahead, she slipped down the hall to Anderson Advertising, where she rapped on the door. "Hello?" She popped her head inside.

Jim Cochran looked up in surprise. "They just cleaned in here last night."

"I know." She did her best to disguise the tremor in her voice. "I just need to take out the trash."

"But—"

"You don't mind, do you?"

"No, but I thought. . ." He glanced back toward the empty trash container.

"I'll just put in fresh bags." She marched confidently into the room and whipped out a box of trash bags. "Never leave a clean room with a dirty trash bag. That's what I always say."

The phone rang. The man turned to answer it, his gaze still following her. "Hello? Oh, hey, John. Glad you called." He shifted his attention to the call. "Did you hear about Chuck?"

Angel listened carefully as she changed the trash bag.

"Yeah. He almost blew it. Got an old lady on the phone and told her. . ."

He glanced quickly in Angel's direction, lowering his voice to a whisper. She took a deep breath and moved to the trashcan in the back office.

Mr. Cochran's voice raised as Angel left the room. "Listen, man, we've got to be more careful. I got an old geezer on the phone yesterday—thought for sure he was an undercover cop or something. He questioned me from every angle then told me he was on to me. We've got to come up with a better script. This is getting too risky."

Good to know, but just hearsay. Nothing that will hold up in court. What I need is— "Evidence." Angel whispered the word as she glanced down at the large oak desk. Sitting right there, atop a messy collage of old soda cans and cigarette butts, she found a stash of credit cards. At least fifty. Maybe more.

With so many, no one will miss one, right? Guilt riddled her. Still, she slipped one out of the pile and dropped it into her bucket. With a whistle, she made her way into the front office once again. Mr. Cochran stared at her suspiciously and hung up the phone just as she prepared to leave.

Angel tried to play it cool. "So you're in advertising, right?"

"Yeah." He leaned back in his chair and looked her over.

"I've got this idea for a commercial. Let me run it by you." She broke into a little ditty about toothpaste then gauged him for his response. "What do you think?"

He shrugged. "Needs work."

"Really?" She moved a little closer to him and tried to act excited. "Could you advise me? I mean, you're the expert."

"Look, I don't have time for this right now."

"Could I come back tomorrow and pick your brain?" she asked. "I'd love to talk to you about the advertising business. I'd really like that."

He grunted. "This isn't a good week."

"What commercials have you done?"

"Excuse me?" He reached up to rub his brow.

"What products? Food? Cosmetics? What sort of companies do you represent?"

He looked more than a little nervous. "What's it to you?"

"Just curious. I want to learn all I can."

"Sure you do. Listen, sister, get on out of here before I call the management company and tell them you're harassing me."

"Are you serious?" Her heart skipped a beat.

"You bet I am. You're taking up time, and time is money. Especially in my line of work."

Angel reached into her bucket for the peace offering inside. "Fine, fine. But before I go, would you like some cookies?"

"What?"

"I brought them for my lunch, but I've got plenty." She pulled out the plate of crumbled cookies and pushed it in his direction. He took one willingly.

"Just because I'm eating this doesn't mean I want you in

here." He gave her a wink and leaned back in his chair, looking her over. " 'Course, you are easy on the eyes."

"And I know my cookies." She bit into one and tried to let his flattery roll off her. *Stay calm, Angel.*

"That you do." He swallowed and reached out for another.

She leaned against the desk and continued to ask him questions. She started by talking about the weather and gradually shifted to more intriguing topics. Who he was. Where he was from. After half a dozen cookies, his answers grew more relaxed.

Lies, clearly, but relaxed lies.

Angel ended up staying in the office a good thirty minutes. When the plate of cookies sat empty, she returned it to her cleaning bucket and smiled. She waved at Mr. Cochran as she headed out of the office. He returned the gesture.

Once in the hallway, she pulled her laptop from her bucket of cleaning supplies and gripped it tightly. She made her way to a nearby closet and slipped inside, leaving the door open a crack to let in some light.

Angel prayed as she typed notes for what was destined to be a great story. *Help Mr. Cochran and those other wicked men to turn from their lives of crime and turn to You. And, Lord, help me to play some role in the lives of women like Ida, who need me.*

She suddenly remembered the credit card she had found inside the office and reached into the bucket to pull it out. *Dennis Morgan.* She looked the card over carefully. *I'll turn this in to the police. They'll find Mr. Morgan, and his credit will be restored. What I'm doing here will be worth it—for Ida, for Mr. Morgan—for all of them.*

Angel's stomach grumbled, and she suddenly realized she hadn't eaten a thing all day—unless you counted two chocolate chip cookies. Just as suddenly she remembered Peter's invitation to dinner at his house and began to panic. She closed the laptop with a snap and headed out of the closet. Tonight she had a date with an angel—and that meant she had some serious clothes shopping to do.

瀚

Peter watched from around the corner as Angel slipped into the small closet. "What is that in her hand?" he whispered to himself. "Looks like a. . ."

A computer.

He stood captivated, watching her every move. She had pulled a blue laptop computer out of her bucket. *Obviously stolen from the office next door. No wonder she carried in such a big bucket. She needed it to stash the goods.* Through a crack in the door, he could make out her actions. Barely. She flipped the laptop open and started to type—slowly at first, then faster and faster, her nails clicking against the keys.

"What in the world?" For a thief, she appeared to be a strong typist. *Should I call the police? Then again, what if I'm wrong? What if. . . ?* Just then she reached into the bucket for something else. *A credit card? Has she resorted to stealing those, too?*

Peter turned toward the elevator. *Father, I pray for Angel right now. I pray that she will come clean—that she'll turn from this life of crime and turn to You.*

All the way down to the first floor he tried to make sense out of what he had just witnessed. Something would have to be done, but what? As he prayed about the matter, the Lord seemed to give some direction.

WAIT. DO NOTHING.

Are you sure, Lord?

JUST WAIT, PETER.

Completely shaken, he headed for the door. Heaven help him if Angel showed up at his home for dinner tonight.

Heaven help them both.

seven

"It's right here, Nardo." Angel pointed at a two-story redwood home with an amazing ocean view. Her heart pounded with a combination of fear and excitement. She had actually made it to the Campbell home. Just in time, too, though tearing her brother away from his work had been difficult. No matter. They were here now. She needed to relax and enjoy the evening.

Nardo let out a whistle as he looked at the house. "This guy of yours must be loaded."

"It's his family's home," she explained. "And it's not like he's my guy. He's not. Not at all." *Not that I would mind having a guy like Peter Campbell.*

"Right, right. Just keep saying that and pretty soon you'll start to believe it. But you look like a million bucks. New dress?"

"Mmm." Angel glanced down at her new black chiffon dress. She had purchased it in her favorite shop in Beverly Hills. It cost a pretty penny but was good quality and would last a long time. Hopefully, if everything went well at work, she would have several occasions to wear it. "Just pull over and let me out, okay?"

"You're not very grateful for the ride, now are you?"

She smiled sheepishly. Her car would be in the shop for another day or so to repair the broken lock. "I'm grateful. Just let me out."

As he pulled over to the curb, the brakes let out a piercing squeal. Angel groaned. "This old car of Dad's—"

"Is a classic! And it's going to be a beauty when I'm done with her. Just you wait and see."

"Okay, okay." She clutched her tiny handbag. "Just let me out. I don't want anyone to see you." After hours of working on his precious car, her older brother remained covered, head to toe, in grease.

"What's wrong? Ashamed of the way I look?"

"Nardo—"

"Come on now."

The car came to a stop, and she reached for the doorknob. "Thanks for the ride." She turned, shocked to find Peter standing just outside the car.

"He looks anxious." Nardo grinned and reached over to give her a playful slug on the upper arm.

"Ow!" She rubbed her arm and slugged him back. "See you later." Angel opened the door carefully, trying to keep the window from slipping out, as it so often did. As Nardo pulled away, tires squealing, she waved good-bye and then looked at Peter with a smile. "Sorry. He's not the best driver."

"I've been meaning to ask you about him." Peter's gaze followed the car as her brother rounded the corner a little too fast.

"Who, Nardo?" She looked up at him nervously. "He's a great guy."

"Does he hurt you?"

"What?" Angel immediately took offense. "Nardo wouldn't hurt a flea."

"I saw him hit you just then—on the arm."

"Oh, that." She laughed. "We play around like that all the time. You know how it is."

"Not really." He took a step toward the large home. She followed at a distance.

Lord, help me to say and do the right things tonight. I don't want to be deceptive. If it's time to tell Peter who I am, what I've been doing, then show me. She tried to make light conversation as they walked. "Great house. Lived here long?"

"Three years," he said. "We moved up from Costa Mesa when my father was promoted."

"I see you're still working there. You must like it."

"I love it. Always have. Nothing pretentious, you know what I mean?"

"Um-hum." She looked at the large house again.

"But what about you?" He asked as he turned to look at her. "You must like the Costa Mesa area pretty well. I mean, you live there, too, right?"

He looked at her suspiciously, and she felt the usual jitters in her stomach. Obviously the time had come to tell the story. The whole story. "Well, actually—"

The front door swung open, and a woman stepped outside. Her blond hair was swept back with a beautiful shell clip, and her hazel eyes shone with excitement. "This must be your friend." She took Angel by the hand.

"Mother, this is Angel. Angel, my mother—Donita Campbell."

Angel squeezed the woman's hand tenderly, surprised at such a warm reception. "Pleased to meet you."

"The pleasure is all mine, I'm sure. Now you two just follow me inside." They made their way through the front door and into a large entryway with a wide curving staircase. "I hope you're not terribly bored tonight, Angel." Donita reached to take her bag. "This is really more of a business dinner. My husband has a client over."

"I'm sure it will be great."

"Well, every time he starts talking about this commercial or that commercial, I just lose interest. I hope it's not too dull for you."

"If it is, I'll jump in and save the day," Peter interjected. "I can usually manage to get Dad to shift back into normal conversation."

"So, your dad does commercials?" Angel was more than a little interested. Perhaps she could discover a few things about how a real advertising firm operated—if she worded her questions correctly.

"Not exactly," Donita explained. "He's an agent. You've probably seen some of his clients in commercials, TV shows, movies. Have you seen the new commercial for Sassy Shampoo? The one where the girl is—"

"Dancing across the living room with the hairbrush in her hand?" She finished the sentence excitedly.

"That's the one. That girl—the one with the red hair—she's his client."

Angel broke into the Sassy Shampoo ditty, and Mrs. Campbell joined in. Peter added the harmony just as his father joined them.

"Peter."

They abruptly stopped singing as Peter answered. "Yes, Father?"

Angel immediately noticed a change in his expression, a more controlled look.

"This is your friend, I take it." Mr. Campbell extended his hand, his lips tight.

She shook it firmly. "Pleased to meet you. I'm Angel Fuentes."

"Angel. Interesting name. I'm Peter Campbell Sr."

"Mr. Campbell."

"I'd like you to meet my client, Mr. Branson Starr." Angel tried not to stare at the shockingly handsome young man who had suddenly appeared in the doorway. He wore a designer suit and sported a tie so white it glistened—even from this distance. It was almost as white as his teeth.

Almost. She nodded in his direction, and Mr. Campbell continued. "I believe Gavin has dinner ready for us. Let's make our way to the dining room, shall we?" He led them into a large room with rich mahogany furnishings. The table was set with exquisite china and large crystal goblets.

Angel studied Mr. Campbell as they sat. He was a tall, foreboding man with a narrow face. Pale. All work and no play, no doubt about that. And he certainly had an eye for spotting talent from the looks of Mr. Starr. But why would Peter's whole disposition change when his father walked into the room?

These were questions worth finding answers to. But right now the most delicious-looking salad she had ever seen was placed in front of her. After little more than two chocolate chip cookies to fend off her hunger today, she couldn't wait to dive in.

&

Peter watched Angel out of the corner of his eye, half afraid she would say something inappropriate in front of his father and half relieved she was here to ease the pressure in the room. His mother seemed content to act as hostess and even paused on several occasions to chat with Angel. They seemed to connect right away. On more than one occasion, his mother caught his eye and winked. He couldn't help but wonder what she would think if she knew the truth. The whole thing made him a nervous wreck.

Peter didn't have to wonder what his father would think if he discovered Angel's identity. He knew without a shadow of a doubt. The man thrived on spending time with the right people and making the right connections. Usually those connections took place on evenings such as this, at stuffy business dinners. These events had always left Peter a little nerve-wracked. The elder Mr. Campbell couldn't seem to leave his work at the office. He also battled an inflated ego, which occasionally put their guests on edge.

But Angel didn't seem to notice. Or, if she did, she didn't seem to mind. On the contrary, she complimented his father on several occasions and spoke to Mr. Starr as if they were old friends.

Mr. Starr. Now there was another story. Peter looked at the fellow suspiciously. He was about as phony as his name. A couple of commercials, one TV sitcom walk-on, and the guy thought he was a superstar. But Angel sure seemed to be paying a lot of attention to him tonight. Of course, he was good-looking. No denying that. Surely she wasn't. . .

Nah. Surely not. Besides, why would he care if Angel showed an interest in Starr?

Was she interested in Starr? For some reason, the very thought worried him. The man seemed glaringly over-ambitious. Angel, clearly, had little ambition. *And she doesn't need to be interested in anyone right now. She needs to be focused on getting her life together. There will be plenty of time for relationships later. And when she is ready, it won't be with a guy like that. Not if I have anything to do with it.*

Not that he had anything to do with it. However, several times during the meal Peter found his attention shifted to Angel. She looked absolutely beautiful in her sleek black gown. It accentuated her dark eyes and olive skin. She was exquisite, right down to her polished nails and black heels. None of this made any sense.

Clearly, Starr had noticed her appearance as well, telling her on several occasions what a knockout she was. She had blushed and thanked him, then politely changed the direction of the conversation.

Peter had missed nothing. But where had the dress come from? That's what he wanted to know. More curious yet, where had she come from? She spoke professionally, clearly impressing both of his parents. They would never have to know he had found her in a Dumpster. She had apparently conquered the art of covering her tracks when she needed to.

"Mmm. This is wonderful, Mrs. Campbell." Peter watched as Angel took a delicate bite of the salmon. "I'd love to have your recipe."

"Oh, I rarely cook, honey," his mother said with a laugh. "But I'll pass your compliments on to our chef."

"Please do." Angel took a larger bite and washed it down with a swallow of water. Peter couldn't take his eyes off her. She had a robust appetite, another puzzle for someone with such a trim figure. Obviously years on the street had left her with curious eating patterns.

As a dessert of fruit and sorbet arrived, Peter finally began to relax. Perhaps his fears concerning Angel were ill-founded. Besides, there seemed to be a real goodness about her that could not be ignored. If only he could balance that with the stolen computer he had seen in her hands just a few short hours ago. Had he completely misunderstood?

As the conversation continued, he joined in, content that the Lord remained in control of this situation. Just as they began to discuss his father's latest client, a woman by the name of Jeanene, something caught his attention. What was that sticking out of Angel's sleeve?

A price tag? As she reached for a strawberry the tag slipped out in full view of everyone in the room.

$395?

Peter's blood began to boil. Every horrible thing he had imagined about Angel was true. She was a thief—and not a very good one, at that. She had stolen a computer, a credit card, and now an expensive dress. Maybe she had paid for it with the bogus credit card and left the tag on so she could return it for cash. Obviously she was skilled at scamming people, but enough was enough. He had to do something—now.

But not in front of his parents.

Peter fought to get Angel's attention. He cleared his throat and dropped his napkin, but nothing seemed to work. Finally he resorted to kicking her under the table.

"Ouch!" She glared at him. He glared back with an accusatory expression. She followed his gaze and immediately reached for her sleeve. Her mouth flew open in despair.

"Are you all right, Angel?" His mother looked concerned.

"Fine. Thank you." Her cheeks turned crimson as she fingered the tag and shoved it up under the sleeve once again.

"You look a little flushed, dear. Are you warm?"

"No, I'm fine." With a little maneuvering, she managed to hide the tag without anyone else at the table noticing.

"Tell us about your work, Angel." Peter directed the question at her with a look that could not be ignored.

She looked up at him nervously.

"My work?"

"Yes, tell us what you do for a living." He had to get to the bottom of this mess, right here, right now.

She bit her lip and shook her head slightly. "There's not much to tell, really. It all started when I went to college at UCLA."

"Great school," his father interjected.

"I went there myself." Branson Starr had to throw his two cents' worth in.

Peter stared at her impatiently. *If she went to UCLA, I'm a Harvard grad.* A little quizzing was in order here. "What did you study?"

"You're a fine one to be asking," his father muttered.

Peter twisted the cloth napkin into knots as he responded. "Dad, you know I'm going to be picking up some ministry classes at Vanguard next semester. I can't help it that I didn't fit in with the secular university crowd. It just wasn't my bag." *He thinks I'm such a disappointment because I didn't get my degree. But he doesn't understand that I have different goals.*

"Hmph." His father turned his attentions to Angel once again. "This young woman was about to tell us her story."

Angel looked about as scared as a kindergartner boarding the school bus for the first time. "Well," she stammered. "At first I studied history. Then later, when that didn't work out, I started working on my—"

"I know just how that goes," Starr interrupted. "I started on a music degree my first year. Second year I switched to business. I finally got it right my third year when I switched to acting." He went off on a long dissertation about his journey to stardom, which only proved to further irritate Peter, who sat in stony silence as the coffee was served. Branson rambled on and on, but Angel never got around to answering the original question.

She was clearly beyond help.

≈

Angel's heart pounded as they stood to leave the dining room. Something had happened to change Peter's attitude toward her, but what? Had the loose price tag really been that much of an embarrassment? Was he so concerned about his father's opinions that a simple slipup could upset him to such a degree?

How prideful could one man be?

Peter Campbell suspected her of something, to be sure. She looked across the table into his blue eyes. They blazed with anger.

Angel fought back tears. When he heard her story, he would understand.

Without a doubt, she must tell him.

Tonight.

eight

"What's your problem?" Angel demanded.

"What's *my* problem?" Peter echoed. "What's *your* problem?"

She stared him down. "I don't have a problem."

"Don't you? I'd say you have a lot of problems." Even in the moonlight, she could see he was prepared for battle. She had felt it coming as they walked out the front door of his house. But why? What in the world had she done to trigger this sort of reaction?

He forged ahead, giving her no time to respond. "Look, I think it's time you and I had a little talk. A serious, get-it-all-out-in-the-open kind of talk. Nothing held back." He grew louder with each word.

Angel shook her head in disbelief. "Calm down, and I'll be happy to talk to you."

"I am calm." He paced back and forth.

"Peter, what's happened to you?" She sat on the front steps, exhausted with his behavior. "You were so nice before, and now you're—"

"I'm what?"

"Well, you're just not yourself."

He blazed ahead, clearly on a roll. "How do you know? You don't know me well enough to make that kind of judgment call."

"Judgment call?" *Lord, what is he talking about?* "I'm just saying that you're acting different now, and I think it's got something to do with your father. Is that it? Am I right?"

"This has nothing to do with my father."

"I think it does," she said. "You're completely different when you're around him. What's up with that?"

"Angel, look. I don't want to get into that right now. To be honest, I just need to know what in the world is up with you."

"Up with me?" She swallowed hard and realized the time had finally come. *This is the moment where I tell him every-thing. But how do I start, Lord?* "Peter, there's a lot to say, but I don't know where to start."

"We'll talk about it as we drive. Then I'm going to come back home and get some much-needed sleep. Maybe things will look better in the morning."

"Maybe *what* will look better?" *Have I really embarrassed him that much?*

"Forget it." He yawned.

Angel's patience had all but worn out. "That's exactly what I want to do," she said. "Forget this whole night. If it's all the same to you, I'd like to go home right now."

"Fine. I'll get my car."

"Don't bother. I'll take a cab." She headed for the front door. "I just need to use your phone."

Peter looked stunned. He spoke in a coarse whisper. "Cabs cost a lot of money, Angel."

She turned to look at him, stunned and offended. "Okay. And your point is?"

His jaw locked in place again. When he did speak, the words seemed well rehearsed. "Do you really think you need to be spending money you don't have?"

"Excuse me?"

"I'm just saying—"

"I heard what you said. But how would you know what I do and don't have?" *Calm down, Angel. He's making that call based on your clothing at Tennyson, that's all.*

"I'd say you've already spent enough for one day, wouldn't you?" He reached to pull the tag out from under her sleeve. She instinctively shoved it back up again.

"That's none of your business."

"I'm making it my business."

Just then the front door opened, and Branson Starr exited. He took a few steps in their direction. "Don't stay up late, you two." He winked.

"I'm not staying at all," Angel mumbled. "The sooner I get out of here the better."

Peter turned toward the front door. "If anyone needs me, I'll be inside calling a cab—which I'll pay for." He closed the front door behind him with a bang.

Angel groaned. "Why does he always have to be the hero?"

"Is that what you're looking for, a hero?" Branson asked.

She shook her head. "Nope. Just a ride."

"I'll be happy to drop you off. Where are you headed?" He took her arm, and she accepted it willingly.

"Into the city, and if you don't mind, I don't either."

"Mind? Of course I don't mind." Branson dove into a lively conversation about his new sports car, and she began to relax a little. Whatever Peter's problem, it was behind her now.

Literally.

She settled into Branson's tiny car and tried to put everything into perspective as he rambled on about fuel efficiency and gas mileage. She nodded occasionally, but nothing seemed to make any sense. Try as she might, the events of the evening just didn't match up. Of course, she didn't know

Peter well enough to make much sense of it all, but something had definitely changed tonight.

But what caused that change? Had she triggered it in some way? Angel yawned and leaned back against the seat as Branson pulled out onto the highway. He talked endlessly about his life, his job, his career, his car. Her ears were weary with listening, but at least he didn't expect much conversation in return.

The trip home took longer than expected. Branson took a wrong turn off Interstate 405, and they ended up in Malibu. An accident, or so she was told. At any rate, by the time she arrived home, her nerves were a jumbled mess. To make matters worse, he tried to kiss her goodnight when they pulled up in front of her house. She was too numb to fight him off. Instead, she turned her head, letting his lips brush her cheek. She entered the house in tears.

Her brother met her at the door. "What happened, Angel? What did he do to you?"

"Nothing, Nardo." She brushed away the tears and headed for the stairs.

He yanked the front door back open. "I'll take care of this."

"No. Close the door. Please. Before you wake up Mom and Dad."

He closed it, then turned to face her with his arms crossed. "Start talking."

"First of all, that's not even Peter out there," Angel explained. "Someone else brought me home." She turned toward the stairs.

Nardo followed behind her. "What happened? Tell me."

"There's nothing to tell. I'm just tired."

"I don't believe you."

"Nardo, please." She sighed and continued walking.

"I know where he lives, Angel. I could go over there and—"

"You wouldn't." She turned to look at him. Her brother didn't have a strong relationship with the Lord, and sometimes his temper still got the better of him.

"I might. What did he do?"

"If I understood it myself, I'd tell you. Trust me." She reached the top of the stairs and headed for her bedroom. "But promise me you won't do anything, Nardo. I'm fine. I really am."

"You promise?" He didn't look convinced.

"I promise."

He shook his head in defeat. "You're too sweet, Angel. You know that? It gets you in trouble every time. If the rest of us didn't take care of you—"

"I know, I know." She forced a smile and entered the safety of her bedroom. Once the door was closed behind her, she melted in a heap on the bed. Tears flowed freely as she reflected on the evening's events, especially Peter's final words.

What did I do to deserve that kind of treatment, Lord? I was kind to Peter—and to his family. I was polite. And yet he treated me like a beggar at his table—someone who wasn't fit to sit beside him. I don't understand.

She dressed for bed, not even taking the usual care to remove her makeup and brush through her hair. All of that could wait until morning. Her sinuses ached with pressure. Probably from all the tears. She had a stuffy head, and her throat tickled. Right now what she needed, what she longed for, was sleep.

What she found, however, was something far different. For hours Angel tossed and turned in the large four-poster bed.

The comforter twisted around her, making her hot. Something had happened at dinner to upset Peter, but what? She played out the conversation over and over again, but nothing came to her.

He seemed so frustrated with me. Why? What did I do? Her mind began to drift to Branson Starr. Peter had shifted his gaze between the two of them several times during the evening. Was it possible? Could he really be jealous?

As preposterous as the idea sounded, it began to grow on her. If Peter had jealousy issues, they were completely unfounded. Guys like Branson were a dime a dozen in L.A. Their heads were a little too big for their bodies. But apparently this revelation meant Peter had feelings for her beyond friendship. How could that be? They had only known each other a few days.

She carefully thought through every prior conversation, trying to remember what she might have said, might have done to encourage his feelings.

Nothing.

Angel punched the pillow with her fist. She couldn't seem to relax and stop her mind from reeling. Her conscience bothered her a little, too. She hadn't been deceitful to Peter, not intentionally, anyway. Clearly she had not disclosed some things, but they were important things—things that could cost her a great job. Things that affected the entire community. If she divulged those things. . .

No. She wouldn't. She couldn't.

Finally, when she could take it no more, Angel switched on the bedside lamp and reached for her Bible. She opened it and quickly thumbed through for something that might bring her comfort. The Word of God always managed to soothe her aching soul, and tonight would be no different.

She settled on a passage in Psalm 77. The first few verses seemed just right for a night such as this. "When I was in distress, I sought the Lord," Angel read aloud, "at night I stretched out untiring hands and my soul refused to be comforted." *Well, that certainly applies.*

She read on, encouraged by the words. "I remembered you, O God, and I groaned; I mused, and my spirit grew faint." She rubbed at her aching forehead then continued reading. "You kept my eyes from closing; I was too troubled to speak." She yawned.

Angel started to lay the Bible down, but something told her to keep looking. Her mind immediately went to the book of James, which she had grown to love in recent weeks. She turned to the first chapter and scanned until her finger landed on a section that spoke to her immediate need.

"If any of you lacks wisdom," she read, "he should ask God, who gives generously to all without finding fault, and it will be given to him. But when he asks, he must believe and not doubt, because he who doubts is like a wave of the sea, blown and tossed by the wind."

The Lord had indeed been generous to Angel. He had brought her into relationship with Himself and delivered her from past fears and hurts. How could she doubt that He remained in control of every area of her life? Had she really been like a wave of the sea, tossed around by the winds life had thrown her way?

Father, forgive me for my doubt.

As soon as the words flitted across her mind, she began to pray in earnest. She prayed about her job situation. She lifted up her family. She prayed for Peter and asked for forgiveness for losing her temper with him earlier. The longer she prayed, the more convicted she felt. Peter couldn't be held responsible for misunderstanding her situation. She had never divulged her full story, as she had planned. That wasn't his fault. It was hers.

He was an amazing man—and a strong Christian. He was a man to be trusted with the truth. She would tell him the truth—every word of it. He would understand and even appreciate her goals to help the elderly. In fact, he might even help her.

Tomorrow she would tell him everything. If she could find him. If not, she would drive to his house and make everything right again. She would tell him why she had dressed as a cleaning woman. She would explain what she was doing in the Dumpster. She would give him as much information about the identity theft story as she felt comfortable sharing. Even if it meant she had to give up her job.

Peter Campbell was a great guy. He came from a good home, a Christian home. That was essential to her. Clearly, he had issues that needed addressing, but so did she. Angel remembered his face as he looked over the edge of the Dumpster. *Such a kind face. Such a good face.*

My angel.

He was quite a man, but had she been looking for a man? Maybe that was the problem. She hadn't been looking.

Then again, maybe the Lord had just dropped one in her lap.

☙

"Calling the police is my best option at this point." Peter talked to himself as he paced in circles around his bedroom. "Of course, if I call them, I'll need to have evidence.

All I have right now is circumstantial."

He paused to rethink the situation. *She's stolen three things that I know of—a laptop, a credit card, and a dress. The problem is, I don't actually have proof of any of those things. Where can I get the proof?* He immediately thought of the large yellow bucket. "If she shows up at Tennyson Towers with the bucket tomorrow, I'll call the police. They'll find everything inside." Except the dress, of course. Heaven only knew what she'd done with the dress.

Peter bit his lip, and the salty taste of blood distracted him from his thoughts for a moment. Angel's situation was sad, certainly, but it did not provide an excuse for thievery. On the other hand, even the worst of criminals could be reasoned with. If they were given a fighting chance and a glimpse at the truth of God's power, they could turn their lives around.

But where would he begin?

Lord, I know now why You gave me this job. I've known all along You wanted me to make a difference in my community. I just didn't know You were going to start with someone as devious as Angel. Give me wisdom, Father. Help me to do only the things You're requiring of me—no more and no less.

Peter felt bad for the person Angel had stolen the credit card from. They would have quite a bill on their hands, from the looks of the tag inside her sleeve. If only he could get his hands on that card. Then he'd know who to call.

The police would know what to do. He contemplated contacting them, in spite of his lack of evidence. The more he calculated, the more uneasy he grew. He continued to pace the room.

WAIT, PETER.

I'm tired of waiting, Lord. Things are only getting worse. Now other people are involved. Other people are being hurt.

WAIT, PETER.

Frustrated, he sat on the edge of his bed. And sat. *Okay, I'm waiting, Lord.*

No response. He yanked the covers down and climbed in, mumbling to himself. After spending one sleepless night already, he needed rest, but would it come?

Funny. When he closed his eyes, all he could see were Angel's deep brown ones staring back into his. Her gentle laugh echoed in his ears, and her sweet smile held him captive once again.

SHE'S MY CHILD, PETER.

He sat up in the bed, ready for an argument with the Almighty. As he did, a host of memories replayed through his mind. Angel in the Dumpster, barely conscious. Angel at the restaurant, shoveling down everything on the menu. Angel at dinner tonight, looking like a beauty queen and impressing his parents beyond belief.

IS ANYTHING BEYOND BELIEF, PETER?

Other memories came just as quickly. Angel typing faster than a pro. Angel talking to his mother as if they were old friends. Angel telling a very believable story about a history class at UCLA.

Lord, is it possible I've misjudged her? If so, show me quickly, Father, and I'll make it right. Before I call the police. Before I take matters into my own hands.

Visions of Angel in that beautiful dress wouldn't leave him. There was a loveliness about her that could not be ignored. She carried an inner beauty, a strength that seemed to rise up from the core of her being. If he didn't know any better, he'd have to say she was no different from the Christian young women he had known.

If he didn't know any better.

nine

"Okay, Angel, here's where the rubber meets the road." Mr. Nigel paced back and forth across his plush office, credit card in hand. He waved it as he spoke. "I tracked down one very anxious Mr. Dennis Morgan. This is his card, all right. Apparently he tossed it in the trash about a month before the expiration date. The bank had already sent him the new one, and he said he never thought to cut this one in half. Just tossed it. People do it every day."

Angel nodded. "Right." She coughed and reached into her purse for a tissue. She had awakened with a terrible sinus headache. To make matters worse, the irritating tickle in the back of her throat had developed into a full-blown hack.

"You're not getting sick on me, are you?" Mr. Nigel's bald head glistened as a ray of sunlight broke through the office blinds. It held her spellbound.

"Just a little cold. I'll be fine." She tucked the tissue back into her purse and focused on him.

A new determination framed his words. "He thinks they got to him by picking through his trash. That means at least one of your guys up at Anderson Advertising must be posing as a trash collector or something. At any rate, they've gotten pretty skilled at going through other people's stuff."

Angel's hand flew to her mouth. *No way. A trash collector?* Her heart picked up speed.

"Mr. Morgan said they, whoever *they* are, used this card to make on-line purchases in the amount of. . .are you ready for this?"

"Go ahead." She braced herself. How bad could it be? After all, it was just one credit card.

"Seven thousand dollars. They bought everything— movies, CDs, books. They even ordered plane tickets—all in the name of Dennis Morgan."

"And the bills?"

"Were sent to him, naturally. Which explains why he's a nervous wreck."

"That's awful."

"Yep. Nearly destroyed his marriage, too. He's had a hard time convincing the Missus he didn't actually charge the stuff. She was ready to leave him." Mr. Nigel picked up the glass paperweight from his desk and rolled it around in his palms.

"That's terrible." *The poor man. On top of everything else, his marriage is falling apart.* Angel coughed again and dug around in her purse for a mint. Nothing.

Mr. Nigel set the paperweight down and focused on his story. "He contacted the fraud department at the bank where the card was issued, but these things take time, or so he's been told. In the meantime, it turns out those creeps took him for a lot more than just what one card could buy. When they went through his trash, they apparently also found his checking account number, social security number, all sorts of things. They've been running up bills all over town using his information."

"Oh my goodness."

"Morgan said he had no clue about that stuff till the clerk at the supermarket refused to take his wife's check—told her she had a history of bouncing them. Wasn't true, of course, but really put her on the spot. That's when she finally realized her husband was telling the truth. Then the family got a call from a wireless phone company demanding $6,500 for unpaid phone service, which someone had taken out in his name, using his social."

"Wow. I'm feeling a little better about removing the card from Anderson's. I don't mind telling you, I felt like I had stolen it."

"Stolen it back, you mean." He continued: "Good news is, the Mister and Missus are back together, and the marriage is out of danger. And, needless to say, Mr. Morgan is particularly thrilled that you've tracked down his card. He's ready to go to the police right away. But I'm trying to talk him into waiting a couple extra days."

"Why wait?"

"What we need here, Angel, is good, hard evidence. Something that will nail these guys to the wall."

"But—"

"I don't mean to belittle the work you've already done." He sighed. "But one credit card doesn't really give us a lot to go on. We need more."

"I understand that, sir. And I'm perfectly willing to—"

"To be honest, I'm a little surprised that this is all you came up with after three days of trying. I hate to go back to our original conversation, but a tougher reporter would have accomplished more by now." He settled his large frame into the chair and gave her an accusing look.

Angel fought against feelings of defeat. "So many things went wrong, Mr. Nigel. But I know I can find more evidence. There was a whole stack of credit cards. Maybe I can get my hands on a few of those."

"That would be helpful, but it's still not enough. We need hard evidence that pins this crime to these particular people. Mr. Morgan is counting on it. Ida Davidson is depending on it."

Angel flinched as he spoke the elderly woman's name.

Mr. Nigel shook his head. "Poor Ida's been without a home for the past month. They robbed her blind, you know."

"I know. You told me. But you never explained how they pulled it off." She took out her notepad and pen, prepared to write down the specifics of Ida's tragic tale. "How did they do it? Maybe her story will give me something to go on." She sniffled, willing herself not to sneeze.

He didn't respond for a moment. When he did speak, his words were slow, deliberate. "Started with a phone call," he said. "They, um, told her she had won a trip to the Bahamas. I think it was the Bahamas. Might have been Tahiti. At any rate, they, uh, they made her give up her social security number to confirm. She also offered up her full name and date of birth."

"Tell me she didn't."

He shook his head. "She gave it, poor thing. The rest is history." He leaned back in his chair.

Angel scribbled frantically. "What do you mean, the rest is history? What exactly did they do?"

"Well." He paused for a moment and looked out the window. "They used the number to open up charge accounts at some of the largest stores in town. She had great credit, which worked to the crooks' advantage. All in all, they took her for over $30,000."

Angel wrote down the information as quickly as she could. "That's the worst story I've ever heard."

"And getting worse every day." Mr. Nigel sat straight up, eyes growing larger as he continued. "The bill collectors started calling. She thought she had to pay them, even though she hadn't charged anything." The veins in his neck bulged, and his words came faster now. "That's what they told her, anyway. So she used up all of her savings trying to get them to leave her alone. In the end, she lost everything. Like I said, she's living in a shelter right now. No place else to go." He sighed and leaned back into his chair once again.

"But, Mr. Nigel, I thought the station was going to help her. I thought they would take care of her."

"That's *your* job, Angel."

"My job?" Her heart seemed to leap into her throat. "Ida won't have a place to stay until I crack this case?"

"If you do your job, she gets to eat. If you don't. . ." He paused at great length. "Well, I hate to think of what will become of her." He shook his head and gazed out the window once again.

Tears formed in Angel's eyes. "My goodness. I had no idea things were so desperate."

"Well, they are, Angel. And others like her are waiting on you to come through for them as well. So you see this is no small matter. If you crack this case wide open—if you're truly the voice of the angels—then you win, KRLA wins, and ultimately the people of Los Angeles win. Do you understand?"

"Yes."

"So what's your plan?"

Angel tried to sound confident as she spoke. "Right now, I'm just getting to know them. I'm trying to figure out how they operate. Picking through the trash isn't their usual M.O., sir. Just a fluke, if you ask me. I've got a feeling they do most of their scamming over the phone." Her words were interrupted by a long fit of coughing. "If I could just find a phone list, I could call some of those people myself and see if they've had any problems. Then we could trace everything back to the list. It will be easy enough to establish where the list came from."

"Of course, this would mean accessing their computers." Mr. Nigel rubbed his chin thoughtfully. "Which means you'll have to go back to their offices at least one more time."

"Yes, sir."

"Are you computer savvy, Angel?"

"Yes, sir. Not sure how I'll crack the password, if they have one, but I'll do my best."

"Your best is all I'm looking for, Angel. It's all Ida and Mr. Morgan are looking for, too. That and some good, solid evidence."

&

"What you need, Peter, is some good, solid evidence." Pastor Robert Bradford spoke forcefully. "It's one thing to accuse someone of stealing, another thing altogether to prove it."

"I know. I know." Peter rolled a black ink pen around in his palm. To be honest, he felt guilty even thinking these things about Angel. "I saw her go in the office and come back out with a computer. That's a start."

Robert shook his head. "Not good enough. Find the computer. Take it to the police. They can check the serial number to see if it's been reported stolen."

"Then there's the matter of the credit card."

"Which could have been her own, for all you know."

"I doubt that, all things considered." Peter slumped back in the chair. "At any rate, I'm headed over to Tennyson Towers to track her movements. I'm convinced I can catch her in a compromising position. When I do, I'll call the police. That's the only thing I can think of. Let them catch her red-handed. Then it's out of my hands."

"Isn't it already?"

"Well, yes," Peter said, "but I meant—" He broke out into a sweat. "There's a crime being committed here, Rob. I can smell it."

"I think that's your aftershave."

Peter groaned.

"You really want my opinion, right?" His friend's voice took on a more serious tone.

"Of course. I wouldn't be here otherwise."

"Then here's my suggestion. Take Angel up to the women's center on Harbor. They've got all sorts of programs to help her get back on her feet again. If that's what she wants. If not, this is really out of your hands. The best you can offer her is your prayers."

"But—"

"And leave her in God's hands. That's easier said than done, I know." Robert looked at him quizzically. "You're the one I'm concerned about."

"Me? What do you mean?"

"I wonder if you're getting in over your head. This girl is really getting to you."

"No way."

"Are you sure your interests in her are purely platonic?" Rob asked. "No romantic interests whatsoever?"

A picture of Angel in that beautiful black dress held Peter captive for a moment before he finally answered. "I don't know. I've never pursued her, if that's what you mean. And if I have feelings for her, they started out as platonic and then changed somewhere along the way. But she's not a believer, Rob. I can't possibly be interested in someone who's not a believer. The woman I have in mind for my wife will be ministry-oriented. She'll be sweet and kind and have a heart for the down-and-out. She'll be someone who lives to *help* people, not steal from them."

"I see your dilemma." The older man smiled. "The girl you've described is nothing like that."

"That's the strange thing," Peter said. "I've seen that side of her, too. She sat at dinner and chatted with my mother like they were old friends. She got along great with my dad. Even I can't do that. She was kind to a total stranger at the dinner table—a client of my father's. I'm just so confused about all of this. But I want to help her. I do. Not for my sake. Not because I want some sort of trophy of my accomplishment as an evangelist, but because I want to know she can be changed. God can turn her life around."

"And then what?"

"What do you mean?"

His friend shrugged. "Then what will you expect from her?"

"Expect? Nothing." Peter hadn't thought about what would happen after the fact. He simply wanted to see Angel clean up her act and become a productive citizen. "Make sure she's planted in a church somewhere?"

"Okay."

"Help her find her God-given gifts. Give her a taste of a better life."

"But you're missing the point, Peter." Robert stood. "Your motives are good, and your heart is pure. That I'm convinced of. But you can't do the work of the Holy Spirit. Even if she does all of the things you hope she'll do, you still have to let go and trust God to do what you can't do. I tell you this to save you from future grief because I know you have a heart to minister to those in the inner city, those in need. You will be used by God to plant many seeds. You'll probably even water a few. But only God can give the increase."

"I know, but—"

"No buts. Do only what the Lord asks of you in each particular case. No more and no less. If you cross the line of service, you'll render yourself useless."

"What do you mean?"

"I mean, God is looking for willing hearts, but He's not looking to hand people over, like projects to be 'fixed.' It doesn't work like that. Be available, but be just as willing to take your hands off completely, should the Lord ask you to."

"Do you think that's what He's asking me now?" He tried to swallow the growing lump in his throat.

"Only God can answer that question, Peter. But it's clear you're emotionally tied to this girl. Maybe the Lord will use you to get Angel on her feet again. Or maybe. . ."

Peter looked up as shame washed over him.

"Maybe He's brought Angel into your life to teach you a thing or two."

ten

Peter hid out in the men's room on the first floor of Tennyson Towers, fidgeting with the keys in his pocket. To steady his nerves, he peeked out the door every few moments. He hoped to catch a glimpse of Angel entering the building. When he found her. . .

Well, he wasn't sure what would happen then, but he would do his best to reason with her. If his patience held out. A few minutes into the wait, his cell phone beeped. It was a text message from his mother: "She's an angel."

Maybe in your eyes, Mom. But you don't know the real Angel. Of course, he didn't either, but he would remedy all of that today. In just a few minutes. He glanced at his watch and sighed.

11:00 a.m.

The minutes turned into an hour, and Peter grew weary with the process. Still he remained, waiting and worrying. A thousand thoughts raced through his mind as he contemplated what could have become of her. Had her rough-looking boyfriend hurt her in some way? Was she in trouble?

Suspecting the worst, he had come today for one last shot at talking some sense into her. He would take her to the women's shelter, if she agreed to go. But first he had to find her. He glanced out the door again and apologized for the umpteenth time as someone tried to squeeze past him.

11:59 a.m.

With a look of sheer determination, Angel entered the lobby, her tennis shoes squeaking against the tile floor as she made her way in haste. Clearly a woman on a mission. That concerned him. Greatly.

She bounded across the lobby, eyes focused. Peter slipped out of the men's room and did his best to follow her. She headed for the stairwell. He opted to take the elevator, knowing where she would end up. *God, whatever she's about to do, watch over her. Guard her. Keep her from evil.*

❧

12:01 p.m.

Lord, protect me. Send Your angels to watch over me, and guard me from evil, Angel prayed as she raced up the stairs of Tennyson Tower. She was nervous about the mission ahead, but nothing would slow her down. Not this time. This time she approached the challenge as a chef would approach a soufflé. She would handle it delicately, and the outcome would be satisfying. For Ida Davidson. For all of Los Angeles' citizens.

Today she carried no bucket, no supplies. She dressed in casual clothes, but nothing that suggested occupation. In short, she came unprepared. And yet in every way prepared. In her pocket she clutched a diskette that would help her access the computer. A keystroker program, or so she had been told by KRLA's computer guru. Pop it in, let the computer boot up off the disk, and a world of information would await—including any passwords. She counted on it.

In her purse, a writeable CD and cell phone also waited. Any valuable information from the computer would be burned to CD, and then she would telephone Mr. Nigel with the necessary information. He would take the ball and run with it, and all of this would be out of her hands.

12:04 p.m.

Armed with a new sense of purpose, Angel knocked on the door of the now-familiar office, though she secretly prayed no one would answer. Time elapsed as she stood in silence. *Thank You, Lord.* The door opened easily. *What did I do to deserve this?*

Once inside, Angel's gaze swept the room for traces of things she might never have seen before. "What could I have missed? Where can I look?" A filing cabinet on the left side of the room caught her attention. She inched her way toward it.

Top drawer. Locked.

Second drawer. Locked.

Third drawer. Open. *Father, help me!* She pressed her hand inside, anxious to pull out evidence to support her story. The story that would save lives, homes, families.

Cheese Puffs. A fistful of stiff, orange Cheese Puffs. Nothing more.

12:07 p.m.

Undaunted, she made her way across the room, anxious to access the computer. She eased into the large leather chair, her heartbeat in sync with the ticking clock to her right. She stifled a sneeze and reached for the mouse. As she did, her hand brushed against a notepad.

Blank.

Currently blank, that is. Upon closer examination, she found the imprint of words that had been written on the sheet above. Angel placed a clean piece of paper over it and rubbed a pencil across it until she could read the words.

They would surely provide evidence.

Pepperoni. Large. $15.95

12:10 p.m.

She pulled the diskette from her pocket and stuck it in the drive on the unfamiliar computer. As it booted up, she prayed. As promised, the computer's files unfolded like a deck of cards before her.

Password included. She wiped her nose with a tissue as she examined the word, making sure she read it correctly.

Scamme.

"Scam me?" Not very creative.

12:14 p.m.

Angel pulled the diskette out of the computer and rebooted. This time it opened up to the usual access area. She quickly entered the password, and the welcome screen loaded. She looked up toward the door and prayed no one would enter.

12:15 p.m.

What am I looking for? Documents, documents. . . there seemed to be a million of them. She clicked the "file" button to her top left and scrolled through all recently opened documents. *What's this one?* She clicked a file titled "masterdb" and waited. Her heart pounded as the document loaded. A database of names, addresses, and phone numbers filled the screen. These guys had everything down to a science—with columns for each stolen item.

Jones in Anaheim SS#896-07-8563.

Marilyn in Costa Mesa, Driver's License #64512784.

Thomas in Riverside, Checking Account #5681-869-813 with full routing number beside it.

Everything they would need to buy the world.

And then some.

12:21 p.m.

Something in her gut told her there was more. Angel scanned the computer's programs, stumbling several times over the web-building software. She ignored it until something in her spirit told her to open the program. When an index page for a self-constructed web site caught her attention, she accessed it right away.

The logo "Free Credit Profile" lit the screen in cyan blue. Underneath, the words "Ever wondered how you can obtain a free copy of your credit report?" appeared. A detailed explanation of how to do so followed. Angel scrolled down, down, down, trying to take it all in. "Enter your social security number here. A free credit report awaits."

No way.

Sure enough, she balanced some of the information against what she had read in the database and put it all together. "They're getting social security numbers from the web, too. This is huge." *Bigger than even Mr. Nigel realizes. This could be the largest identity theft ring in California's history.*

12:24 p.m.

Curiosity aroused, Angel searched for more. She signed on-line, using the same password: scamme.

Just a lucky guess.

As she attempted to access mail files, she ran into a small problem—an instant message from someone with the name "smarterthanu." The incoming ring nearly shot her out of the large leather seat. "Nick, is that you?" the message read.

Angel's hands shook. She tapped her fingers on the desk as she stared at the nameplate before her. Jim Cochran. "Guess we'll have to start calling you Nick," she mumbled.

"Nick, you on?" Whoever it was, was mighty impatient.

"I'm here." She typed the words nervously, stopping once to correct a spelling error.

"Listen, I need a favor."

"Yeah?" Her heartbeat drummed in her ears, making it difficult to concentrate.

"Check our card stock supply, will you? I've got over two hundred orders this afternoon, and these guys are in a hurry."

Two hundred orders? For what? She contemplated her next question. If answered, it could lead police directly to the bad guys. "Where did you say you are again?"

"Outside immigration. I told you that before I left this morning. You all right, man?"

"Yeah. Just tired," she typed. "Hang on a minute." She looked around the office for card stock but couldn't find a trace of any.

"No card stock," she typed.

"Figures. I'll stop by the office supply on the way back. See you in a few minutes."

A few minutes? She glanced at her watch for the umpteenth time. When she looked back up, he had signed off.

12:29 p.m.

Angel went back to the task at hand, quickly accessing the "old mail" files. Most of it appeared to be junk mail, but she finally stumbled across a gold mine—hundreds of e-mails from Internet users, all with personal credit card information attached. *Why? Why would they so willingly give up private information?*

She scrolled through the "sent" folder, startled to find one piece of mail that had been sent out to over a thousand Internet users. She scanned it, barely able to believe what she read. "Your Internet Account Information needs to be updated." *I've gotten these myself!*

She sneezed. After a quick dab with the tissue, Angel continued to scroll through the letter. "The credit card you used to sign up for this account is either invalid or expired. The information must be reentered to keep your account active."

That would explain the hundreds of responses they had received.

And hundreds of credit card numbers they had obtained. She glanced back through some of the responses, gathering names, and then did a search of the database to match names. "Bingo."

12:37 p.m. *Better hurry.*

She pulled the writable CD from her purse and popped it into the CD-ROM drive. Nothing happened. On her computer at home, a blank CD always opened the software on its own. But not here. Frustrated, she tore through every software program she could find. There were a couple of unfamiliar ones on the computer, but none seemed to be related to the mysterious drive.

Does this thing even have a CD burner? She looked the machine over carefully. Fortunately, all the necessary hardware was there—but no software to operate it. She raced across the Internet, looking for a trial version of the software she used at home.

12:46 p.m.

By the time she had the software downloaded and installed, Angel felt as if she would be sick. She quickly burned files, dragging several hundred megabytes' worth to the CD. She would have to look through it all more carefully when she got back to the office. Right now she had to. . .

A sound at the door shot her out of the leather seat. *They're back. God, help me!* She quickly shut off the computer and ran toward the back office. *Where do I go?* She tried a closet door in the far right corner of the room. Locked. No, not locked. Just stuck. She gave it a hard yank, and the door opened with a squeak.

Angel slipped inside the small closet, at once butting up against a piece of machinery just as she heard the front office door opening. She leaned back against the metal object, heart racing madly.

Only then did she realize she had left the CD in the computer.

No time to worry about that now. She tried to make out the voices of the men. From this distance, they were difficult to understand. She reached for her cell phone to dial KRLA. *Mr. Nigel will know what to do.* She stared in silent disbelief at the phone.

Battery. Dead.

Now she could make out the voices.

"What do you mean you talked to me on-line? I've been out of the office for over an hour." *Mr. Cochran's voice. Or rather, Nick's.*

"No way, man. I've got the card stock right here. I bought it because you told me we needed it."

"We've got a closet full of the stuff."

"I'm telling you—" Angry now, the men were easier to hear, though that didn't pacify Angel much.

"What have you done to my computer?" When she heard Nick's angry words, she felt as if her heart would plummet to her toes.

"I never touched it. I know how you feel about that."

"You loaded software onto my computer? What's your problem?" Dead silence permeated the dark closet for a moment or two, and then Angel heard shuffling in the front office.

"I told you they were on to us, Nick. I've been feeling it for days."

"Well, someone's messed with my computer, and I seriously doubt it's the cops. Why do you always have to lie to me?"

"The FBI, man. They've hacked our computer. That must've been them talking to me on-line awhile ago."

"Is this their CD, too?"

"I never saw it before, Nick. I swear. . ."

Angel shook her head, completely defeated. Only then did the tickle in her nose present a problem. She fought against it. Tried everything to stop it. In the end, she had to give in to it.

"What was that?" The voices moved her way. They were in the back room now.

She heard them open the closet on the other side of the room. In an act of sheer desperation Angel shot out of the closet and sprinted toward the front office. Nick turned and called out just as she reached the computer. The CD-ROM drive stood open, with the evidence still right there, within her grasp.

And grasp it she did.

With the CD firmly clutched in her hand, she slipped out the front door of the office. She could hear Nick close on her heels as she ran. If she could just make it to the elevator, she would be safe. She turned back for one quick look.

From out of nowhere he came.

Peter Campbell.

My angel!

eleven

"Angel, stop!" Peter reached out to grab her, though she seemed to recoil at his touch. Her breathless words frightened him.

"I can't. Not right now!"

From down the hallway, a tall man with dark hair raced toward them. His movements confirmed Peter's worst fears. Angel had obviously been caught in the act of stealing. But what had she taken this time?

"Peter, let me go." She twisted loose from his grasp and headed for the elevator. She pushed the button repeatedly as she waited. In her hand she clutched a CD of some sort. Not much of a find, if that's all she had managed to lift.

He turned his attentions to the tall man, who fought to catch his breath as he approached. He looked agitated. Then again, who could blame him?

"It's okay," Peter whispered. "I've already called the police. They're probably waiting downstairs right now."

"You did what?" The fellow's expression changed immediately.

"This will all be over soon," Peter said. The man's neck turned red. He slapped himself in the head and sprinted back toward the office.

Odd reaction.

The elevator door opened with a "ding," and Angel dove inside. With an outstretched arm, Peter held the door. "I want to help you, but first you have to help yourself. That's all anyone is asking."

She shook her head and shoved the CD into her purse. "Peter, what *are* you talking about?"

"You know perfectly well what I'm talking about, Angel, and it's about time you came clean."

"Came clean?" She glanced at her watch. "Just let me go, Peter. Please. I have work to do."

"It *will* take work to make all of this right again. But in the end it will be worth it."

She shook her head once again. "I don't have a clue what you're talking about. But standing there all day with the door open won't accomplish anything. Come with me. Please. I need help."

Those were all the words he needed to hear. He practically leapt into the elevator with her. Angel slumped against the wall, drawing deep breaths.

"What were you doing in that man's office?" He looked her squarely in the eye. *Those beautiful eyes.*

She countered his stare. "Working. But my job's not done yet. So as soon as I get downstairs, I've got to get out of here."

"Angel, you can't. It's not that easy."

"Nothing about this has been easy," she said. "But it's almost over now. I've wanted to talk to you about it for days, but I didn't know if I could trust you. I thought you were on their side."

"I *am* on their side. That's what I'm trying to say."

The corners of her lips turned down and her eyes filled with tears. "You're what?"

His heart twisted. "Why do you look so surprised?"

"Don't I have a right to be?"

"Not—not really." Surely she knew he was a Christian. He had made that very clear days ago. A Christian would have to side with those who were in the right, even if it meant hurting her feelings.

Her face turned pale, and she took a step away from him. "You? You're the trash guy?"

"I thought we had already established that."

"But I mean—you're working for them?" She gazed into his eyes with the look of one who had been betrayed.

"I want to help them," he said. "But I want to help you, too." Couldn't she see that?

The elevator door opened, and a lobby full of people stood before them. Peter looked around for someone, anyone, in a Costa Mesa police uniform. No one. Angel raced toward the back door, shoes squeaking against the tile floor. Peter reached to touch her shoulder. "Stop, please. Let's talk." She kept walking.

When she spoke, her words were rushed, breathless. "We *can* talk. Just not here. Not now. Come with me, and I'll explain everything."

"Where are we going?"

"Into town." She headed for a familiar silver sports car.

No! Not this again. He wouldn't let it happen. He couldn't. "I can't let you take that car." She pulled a set of keys out of her purse. *Where did those come from?*

Angel shot a nervous glance up to the fourth floor before she answered. "Peter, you're talking crazy." She pushed a button on the remote, and he heard the locks click. "Hop in."

"I'm not getting in there, and you're not either."

She climbed into the car, ignoring his pleas. "Peter, I don't know what your problem is."

"Don't do this, Angel." She turned the ignition, and the engine started with a gentle hum.

"I'm telling you, I know what I'm doing." Desperation filled her eyes. "But I can't make you come with me. And after what you said in there, I can't even trust you anyway." She slammed the door and backed out of the parking space.

Peter watched, mystified, as she pulled out of the parking lot. The silver sports car very nearly struck another vehicle as it entered Tennyson Towers. A Costa Mesa police car. He waved his arms trying to flag the officer. He pointed down Harbor in Angel's direction. The patrol car came to a stop beside him.

The officer rolled down his window. "Can I help you?"

"Yes," Peter said. "I'm the one who called. The girl I told you about—the one who's been stealing from the offices here—she just took off in that silver sports car. The one that almost hit you."

"Stolen?"

"I—I think so." He had no way to prove that, but it just made sense.

"You got the plate number?" The officer reached for a notepad.

"No. Sorry."

"I'll need a full description of the vehicle, then."

Peter gave the officer as many details as he could recall. Then he described Angel.

"This is really not that big of a deal." The officer snapped his notepad closed. "Someone is bound to come out of the building eventually looking for that car. I'm sure they'll call us. When someone has been victimized, they always call, trust me." He thanked Peter for the information and reached for the gearshift.

"You're not leaving, are you? I have a witness upstairs who

can give you all the information you'll need to nail this girl once you track her down. If you'll come with me."

"I hope you know what you're talking about," the policeman said as he got out of his patrol car.

"Sir, I've got this coffin nailed shut." Peter escorted the impatient officer up to the fourth floor and rapped on the door of Anderson Advertising Firm. The tall fellow answered the door. Everything would be solved momentarily. "The police are here," Peter said. "They have a few questions about the girl."

"The girl?" The man's eyebrows lifted slightly. "What girl?"

What's wrong with this guy? And why does he look so nervous? "The one you were chasing down the hall a few minutes ago."

The officer cleared his throat as he pulled out his pen and notepad once again. "We'll need a list of everything she's stolen."

"Stolen?" The tall man looked stunned. "I don't have a clue what you're talking about."

❧

Angel cried all the way to Los Angeles. With the traffic jam on I-405, she had plenty of time to empty herself of emotion. Her tears were a mix of relief and sheer frustration. She had managed to get the necessary evidence to crack the case, even sparing her own life in the process. But Peter. He had confessed to working with those awful men. *Lord, how could I have been so wrong about him?*

She allowed herself to play back through the conversations over the past few days as she searched for clues, flaws in his character.

Nothing. Unless you counted the weird incident at his house that night.

And the part where he leaned over to whisper something into Nick's ear.

And the part where he showed up, coincidentally, at the Dumpster that first day to rescue her. *If all that's true, then why did he take me to lunch?* The answer smacked of painful truth. *He was already on to me. He knew why I was there. They sent him to keep tabs on me.*

The more she thought about it, the more obvious it became. Peter Campbell presented himself as a model citizen, but that was clearly just a cover. On the inside, he was as evil as those men upstairs. His crooked smile and dimples were all part of a bigger plan of deception. Danger and evil lurked behind his bright blue eyes.

Shame washed over Angel as she acknowledged her vulnerability. Once again, she had been taken. Mr. Nigel was right. Her journalism professor was right. They were all right. *If he's really as wicked as I think he is, then everything— everyone—has been part of it. That means his parents were in on it, too.*

She tried to think back through the conversation at their home. Donita Campbell was just a little too stiff, too perfect. Her husband—if he really was her husband—wasn't a very good actor. He hadn't impressed her much. And that other fellow, Branson Starr. What kind of name was that? Completely contrived. *I can't believe I fell for it.*

Just like I fell for Peter.

The truth of her feelings came from out of nowhere. The reason this hurt so badly, the reason she felt it so deeply, was because she had given a piece of her heart to Peter Campbell. *My angel is a wolf in sheep's clothing.*

Maybe the whole thing had been a lie. Maybe that house in

Newport Beach was purchased with dirty money. Maybe. . . Her mind raced. All sorts of scenarios lit her imagination on fire. Of course, Branson had offered to drive her home. Peter's family had probably set that up. She struggled with the implications of that. They knew where she lived. She had placed her entire family in danger.

How would she explain all of this to her father? *Maybe we'll have to go back to Ensenada. Maybe Uncle Mario can take over the restaurant. Maybe. . .*

As He had done so many times over the past few days, the Lord again reminded her of a familiar verse from the book of James.

Blessed is the man who perseveres under trial, because when he has stood the test, he will receive the crown of life that God has promised to those who love him.

As she pulled into the parking lot of KRLA, Angel forced herself to focus on the task at hand. If she didn't get this CD into Mr. Nigel's hand soon, she would lose her job and more of Los Angeles' elderly would lose their money.

twelve

"You haven't been yourself lately, honey. Is everything okay?"

Peter glanced up at his mother as she seated herself next to him at the poolside. She dipped her feet in the water, her bright pink toenails shimmering under the crystal clear water.

"Yeah," he mumbled.

She splashed water on him, an attempt at playfulness. She obviously wanted his attention. But he didn't want to give it. Not today. He just wanted to be left alone.

She cleared her throat. Peter finally gave a bit of a response. "I'm fine." He slipped down the blue tiled wall and inched his way into the chilly water.

She made the same face she always made when she didn't get her way. "Does this have something to do with the girl?"

"The girl?" He ducked under the water, doing all he could to avoid his mother's stare. As he came up, he shook the excess water from his hair and formulated a way out of this conversation. "I'm going to swim a few laps, Mom. Can we talk later?" He took off, not waiting for her response. By the time he got to the end of the pool and back, she had disappeared.

For a while anyway. A few minutes later she arrived in a bright yellow swimsuit with matching goggles.

"I felt like taking a little dip myself." She gingerly stepped into the water, making faces as the cold liquid enveloped her.

"Hope you don't mind."

Peter grunted and went back to swimming laps. He didn't feel like talking to anyone right now. Except perhaps Angel.

Nearly twenty-four hours had elapsed since their parting, and so many questions remained unanswered in Peter's mind. What was her story—her real story? Why had that dark-haired guy at Tennyson Towers denied her existence? Why did she have a key to the silver sports car? Why did she react so strongly to his comments about siding with those she had been taking advantage of?

Why did she look so scared?

"Yoo-hoo. Could you rejoin me on the planet?" His mother tapped him on the shoulder.

"I'm—I'm here." He ducked his head beneath the water again and stayed under as long as his lungs would allow. When he finally did emerge to catch his breath, Peter couldn't avoid his mother's words.

"The truth will come out, you know. It always does."

He sighed. "It's the truth that worries me."

"What do you mean?"

"I haven't been hearing a lot of it lately, that's all. In fact, it's getting pretty hard to tell the truth from a lie these days."

"Just tell me what's on your mind," she urged. "I can take it, whatever it is. Besides, I know it's got something to do with Angel."

"Mom, I just don't know."

She laughed. "No guy ever knows how to talk about women. It's not an easy subject. But maybe I can help." She looked genuinely interested, and he couldn't help but feel a little guilty rejecting her help.

Peter ran his fingers through his matted hair and pulled his weight up onto the side of the pool. "This is beyond help."

"Nothing is beyond help." She engaged him in a locked stare. "Not beyond God's help, at any rate."

"I know that. And I've been asking, but I don't seem to be getting anywhere."

"Could you be more specific?"

I'M GIVING YOU AN OPPORTUNITY, SON. USE IT.

Peter heard the words as if they had thundered out of heaven itself. He tried to swallow the lump in his throat before delving into the story. The whole story.

He started slowly and then picked up speed as he went along. He told his mother how and where he and Angel had met. He shared the humorous details of how she smelled that first day at the restaurant. He relayed how thrilled he had been to see her at their house looking so beautiful. He told his mother how it made him feel when Branson Starr took such an interest in Angel, and how badly the evening had ended.

Peter told her the whole, awful story—of calling the police, of the man in the office. Everything.

She listened quietly, and he was unable to read anything from her expression. "You know," she said, "I have a sneaking suspicion this isn't quite what you think it is."

"What do you mean?"

"I've got pretty good discernment. And from the little bit of time I've spent with Angel, I'd have to say she's the real thing. She's well-bred, has great manners, and clearly connects with you on more than just an emotional level. That's not just a mother's intuition talking." She sat next to him.

"But, Mom, you haven't seen the other side of her. She can

be sneaky and conniving and—"

"I hear what you're saying, but I'm sure you're missing something. I know you don't want to hear this, but I feel like you're off base this time, honey. Maybe you've made her out to be all of these things so that you can rush in and rescue her. Is that a possibility?"

That's the same thing Rob accused me of. "I'm not sure I'd put it quite like that."

"Listen." His mother's voice trembled a bit. "I know what you're up against. I know the kind of man you want to be and the kind of man you're trying so hard not to be."

Peter sat in stunned silence. *How could she possibly know?*

"You want to be a man of God, someone who cares for people. You've been like that since you were a kid. You always wanted me to stop and give money to every homeless man on the street."

"Nothing wrong with that," he muttered.

"No. Nothing at all. But the task is so great, Peter, and you've taken it all on yourself. And when you took that job as a trash collector—"

"What about it?"

She paused and seemed to focus on her pink manicured nails. "Your father had offered you such a nice position at the agency," she said finally. "You could have had anything you wanted. But you chose the job in Costa Mesa."

"And you're ashamed of that?" He put his hand up to block the sun's glare.

"No, Peter. Nothing could be further from the truth. I was extremely proud of you, because I knew God could use you there. And He has. I'm just asking you to check your motivations, that's all."

He shifted his position, unnerved by the direction this conversation was taking.

"I'm wondering why it's so important to distance yourself from your father in every situation. Are you trying to prove something to him?"

Her words stung. Peter felt goose bumps rise on his arms. "What do you mean?"

"Your father may struggle with pride at times, but that doesn't make him a bad man. He's just a man. Like you."

Not like me. We're nothing alike.

Her eyes took on a faraway look. "When your father and I first got married, we had nothing. We lived in a tiny apartment in Riverside. Our grocery budget was twenty dollars a week, if that gives you any indication of how things were."

This was a new story, one that Peter couldn't help but pay attention to.

"Your dad worked for the school district back then. He drove a bus."

No way.

"Your grandfather didn't make things easy on us, that's for sure. He never had a penny to his name, and yet his quest for money always seemed to drive him. He never found what he was looking for, and he died in debt—a bitter man."

"Wow," Peter said. "I always knew he had a chip on his shoulder, but I couldn't figure him out."

"No one could," she continued. "Your grandfather had more pride than a lot of rich men I've known. For some reason, and I could never figure out why this was, he always accused your father of being a failure. Nothing your dad ever tried was good enough. Grandpa Joe said he'd never make anything out of his life. So your dad decided, out of spitefulness, I might add, to prove your grandfather wrong."

He proved him wrong, all right.

. "Your grandfather never lived to see the success your father made of himself, so they both lost out."

"Hmm."

"The sad irony is, I think you want to be as opposite from your father as he wanted to be from his. But the truth is, doing anything out of spite—or to make a point—is doing something for the wrong reason. No matter how noble. No matter how godly."

Peter kept his gaze on the water. It rippled beneath his feet as he moved them back and forth.

"And whether you know it or not," she added with a sly smile, "your father is one of the most giving men I know."

"Giving?"

"You don't see everything, Peter. But there are things your father has done that others know nothing about."

"Such as?" Curiosity had the better of him now.

"Well, take the new gym at the church, for instance."

Peter shrugged. "What about it?"

"Remember that 'unnamed benefactor' Pastor Rob thanked from the pulpit just before the groundbreaking?"

"Are you saying. . . ?"

"I am. And the street ministry. I guess you never stopped to think about who funded that feeding center you work at. It takes a lot of money to get a project like that off the ground. They needed thousands of dollars to get the kitchen area renovated and up to city code. And then there was the matter of hiring a permanent staff to guide those of you who volunteered your services."

I had no idea. Peter shook his head in shame.

"There are a thousand other things I could tell you," his mother continued. "But at least hear this, Peter. A lot of what you're interpreting as pride in your father is simply fear. He's afraid of letting his guard down and having others see that he's vulnerable. A lot of men are like that."

"And some are just the opposite." Peter stared at the water, the truth suddenly hitting him.

"Yes. They are. But both are just men." She cleared her throat, and the silence became almost overwhelming.

"Right." The word came out as a soft whisper.

"But, Angel," his mother continued, "now that's another story altogether. She's not a man, is she?"

"Definitely not." Peter smiled as the memory of Angel in that black dress reignited him.

She grinned. "Definitely not."

"So what would you do?" he asked. "I mean, if you were me."

"That's easy." She stood and turned toward the house. "I'd find her and get to the bottom of all this." She pulled the towel tighter around her. "Then I'd do my best to hold onto her as long as God would allow."

❧

Angel looked up as Mr. Nigel stepped into her cubicle at KRLA. His bulk nearly filled the tiny space to overflowing. "So, do you feel better now that you've slept?" he asked.

She yawned her response. Truth be told, she hadn't slept much. Between the tears and the joy, there had been little time.

"I've had some time to look over the CD." He pulled up a metal chair and eased himself into it. "You've hit the jackpot, Angel. Great work."

"Thank you, sir." She felt her cheeks flush. *Swallow that pride, girl.*

"We've got our legal analysts looking at the files now. The police have been contacted, but they're probably going to wait until tomorrow before they make their move. They decided to call in the FBI."

"Really?"

"Yep. Whenever I get word an arrest is about to go down, I'll send a news crew out there to get some footage."

"Do I have to—?"

"No, kid. You've done enough. You can relax now. We need you right here. We'll mix and match your live report here at the studio with any clips they bring back. In the meantime, put together the strongest story you can."

She took a deep breath and rested against the back of the chair. "I've already started it."

"Atta girl."

As she watched her boss walk away, Angel shifted her thoughts to Peter Campbell. She contemplated their last run-in. Despite her best research, she couldn't seem to link him in any way to Nick and the others. *Just one more piece of the puzzle yet to be solved.*

thirteen

"What are you up to, honey?"

Angel looked up as her mother appeared in the doorway. She turned her attentions from the laptop just long enough to give a quick answer. "Finishing my story."

"Oh, you're done with all of that secretive stuff, then?" A look of relief washed over her face.

"Yes." Angel paused to stretch and gaze lovingly at her mother. "As soon as I get this written, anyway. It's going to be aired this evening at five o'clock."

"Really?" Her mother clasped her hands together. "You're going to be on the news?"

"Yes. Hopefully." She turned back to the computer and typed a couple of words. She hit the backspace key, erasing them almost immediately.

Nothing she wrote today seemed to feel right or to do this story justice. She had to work hard to make this piece the absolute best it could be. KRLA's reputation was at stake, but so was her own.

"Can I call my friends and tell them?" Her mother looked nearly as excited as Angel felt.

"Sure." Why not let her mother enjoy the moment? She had done well over the past several days—not once asking for details, though Angel knew she had been concerned.

"Can you give me specifics, now that everything is said and done?"

"Are you sure you don't want to wait to hear it on the evening news?"

"I'm sure." Her mother sat on the edge of the bed, hands folded in her lap.

Angel began to share the week's events, doing her best not to read too much into her mother's reactions. She told her everything.

Except the part about Peter Campbell. For some reason, she couldn't seem to make herself tell that part. Angel would never be able to hide her true feelings for Peter from her mother. *What are my feelings for Peter?*

"You took a lot of risks, honey," were the only words her mother offered when all the information regarding the identity thieves had been told.

"I know. But it will be worth it, Mama." She then dove into the story of Ida Davidson. Her mother shook her head in disbelief. "That's just terrible."

"I know," Angel said. "But I feel so good about the fact that I could help her. So you see, it was all worth it."

"I agree," her mother said with a smile. "And when I think about the fact that you've spared the elderly citizens of Los Angeles further tragedy, I could just cry." True to form, her eyes filled with tears.

"It's made all of the risk worthwhile," Angel said with a sigh.

For a moment, the two sat in silence, staring at one another. Finally, Angel's mother reached to embrace her. "I don't know if your father and I have expressed this adequately, but we're really proud of you. Maybe we haven't always shown it, but we are."

Angel's heart swelled. "That means a lot to me."

"And now you're going to be on television!"

"I am." She turned back to the laptop, nervously tapping the keys. "If I get this story finished, I mean."

"I'll leave you alone." Her mother reached for the door. "I'm just glad it's all over. Your father and I have been praying for you."

"I know, Mom," she said. "I've felt those prayers, and I'm thankful. Trust me."

She turned her attentions fully back to the story. She hadn't written much yet, just a few short sentences. How could she possibly take all the events of the past week and boil them down into one four-minute segment? Impossible.

And yet she must. Angel carefully crafted her words, wanting to share details without delving into overkill. No point boring the television audience with unnecessary details.

She sighed as she reflected on Ida Davidson. *I hope she's watching tonight. I hope they've told her.* Somewhere in Los Angeles an eighty-three-year-old grandmother would soon be vindicated.

If this story ever got written. She glanced at her watch: 9:43 a.m. *Finish the story. Deliver the story.*

The telephone rang. She ignored it, hoping someone else would pick it up. Within seconds, her mother reappeared at her door, eyes large with excitement. "It's Mr. Nigel from your work. He says it's very important."

Angel groaned. *He's wanting to make sure the story is written, and I can't seem to put two words together.* She picked up the receiver. "Hello?"

"Angel? Listen, I've got an update." Mr. Nigel sounded rushed.

"Yes?" She accidentally knocked over a diet soda, spilling it all over her notes. Her mother rushed in to help clean up the mess as she listened to his breathless words.

"I've just received word the arrest is under way in Costa Mesa," he said. "I've got Joe Shockey, one of our best cameramen, out there now. Good news is, none of the other stations will get live coverage. From what I hear, no one has nosed out any details but KRLA. Joe says he'll call when he's got the footage. By the way, how's your story coming?"

"Uh, great." She swallowed hard.

"Good. We'll tie it all together when you get up here. In the meantime, could you fax me a copy when you're done with it? Say, around noon?"

"Sure."

"Oh, I need to let you know one thing," Mr. Nigel added. "That blond guy, the trash collector?"

"Peter Campbell?" Her heart raced.

"He's clean."

"I beg your pardon?" she gasped.

"I mean, he's clean," Mr. Nigel continued. "Well, as clean as any real trash collector could be. He works for the City of Costa Mesa. That Newport Beach address you gave me is legit. The guy works at a homeless shelter when he's not dumping trash. Mom's a country club socialite. Dad's a—"

"An agent in L.A." She finished the sentence for him.

"Right. Well, anyway, your theory about Peter Campbell's involvement was off base, but other than that you were right on target. Those other guys are a major news story. Maybe the biggest of the year for this area. The police say there's enough information to make a great case, thanks to your legwork. This is really something, Angel."

"Wonderful!"

"You've done us proud at KRLA, and I think I can assure

you a pretty long run with the station if you keep going like this."

"Oh, Mr. Nigel. I'm so grateful." Her hard work had paid off!

He picked up the pace again. "I've got to get off here so I can make a couple of calls. Get me that story by noon, okay?"

"Yes. Of course." She heard a click as he hung up the phone.

With trembling hands, Angel hung up the phone. Peter Campbell wasn't a liar or a crook. He was all he had made himself out to be. She replayed the entire week's events over in her mind, trying to make some sense of his actions. Nothing made any sense.

Then again, neither would her story if she didn't get busy writing it. When Angel looked at her watch, she realized forty-five minutes had passed. She turned her attention back to the screen and typed like a woman possessed.

೩

Peter drove like a man in a trance. He reflected on many things as he made his way down the familiar stretch of Harbor Boulevard. His misconceptions about his father were first and foremost in his mind. They had shaped so many other decisions, so many other ideas and opinions. To think he had been wrong about the man, on every level, seemed inconceivable. And yet perhaps he had been.

For years, he had avoided a relationship with his dad, but why? As soon as he dared ask himself the question, Peter knew the answer. All of their struggles could be traced back to an incident in his childhood when he was twelve, after his father had accumulated all the money and respect a man could ever want or need.

It had happened on a Sunday morning after church.

Peter's best friend, Nick Morton, had lingered behind in the junior high Sunday school room after all the others left. When Peter went back in to look for him, he found his friend in tears. Nick explained that his family was about to lose their home. Though his best friend hadn't divulged all the information, Peter remembered it had something to do with gambling debts his father acquired in Vegas.

Peter knew just what to do. The Nortons needed money. His father had lots of money. If his dad would just do the right thing and take care of this family in need, everything would be solved. Nick could stay here, and Mr. Morton would come to know the Lord.

But Peter's father refused. *"It's not my place,"* he had said.

"Then whose is it?" Peter still remembered the question. " 'Whatever you did for one of the least of these brothers of mine,' " he quoted.

His father had been firm on the matter. "There are some things you just don't understand, Peter. You can't save everyone."

Those words rang in his ears as Peter looked up and saw Tennyson Towers in the distance. *You can't save everyone.*

Nick's father had ended up in prison, and Nick all but disappeared. Peter would never know if his dad's help might have changed the course of history, but he couldn't help seeing a little of his father's side in it now.

For years he had accused his father of being a prideful man, and yet now Peter had to admit his own pride had surfaced. In trying to prove his dad wrong, he had thrown his own spiritual life out of balance and nearly lost the relationship with his father as well.

Funny how pride could reverse itself.

He had missed the truth in his father's words for years, but it shone like a beacon now. *Lord, I know You didn't put me here to fix every problem I run across. Show me when and how to minister to people, and help me not to assume. Give me balance, Lord.*

His thoughts lingered a moment on Angel. He didn't feel a sense of release from that situation, and yet he knew he must give her over to God in order for the Lord to move. Without a personal experience of her own, she might never understand the love and acceptance of the Lord he took for granted. *How did that love get so mixed up with my own feelings?*

Plagued with guilt, Peter glanced at his watch. It was almost noon. One more stop and he would be finished for the day. This afternoon he would head down to the feeding center to help with the evening's street feed and church service. It would keep his mind off the craziness of the week.

And off of a beautiful dark-haired Angel.

He braced himself as he approached Tennyson Towers. How could he keep coming here day in and day out without desiring a glimpse of that beautiful face? How would he ever press her from his memory? *How will I ever get past what I'm feeling?*

It wasn't like he hadn't tried, after all. Peter had spent hours contemplating all that his mother and pastor had said. He had spent even more time analyzing what he felt God was now saying. None of it made him feel much better about the situation. For all his concerns and all his suspicions, warranted or not, he couldn't lay aside the idea that he was supposed to be involved in Angel's life in some way. But he would probably never see her again.

He pulled into the parking lot and numbly made his way to the back of the building. *Just get through this. Every day it will get a little easier.*

As he downshifted and approached the familiar Dumpster, he tried to remain focused. He engaged the truck's arms and began to lift the metal trash unit into the air. He leaned back against his seat and turned on the radio.

Just as Peter started to relax, a noise to his right caught his attention. The parking lot suddenly filled with patrol cars. They swarmed in like locusts. The dizzying scene mesmerized him. "What in the world?" Peter momentarily left the Dumpster in midair as he watched the flurry of activity. *Something big is going on. But what?*

Officers streamed from the vehicles and entered the building. Dozens of them.

Stay focused.

Peter brought the Dumpster back down to the ground with a loud thud. He withdrew the metal arms and turned the vehicle off. Then he turned his full attention to the building.

A large white van bearing the logo "KRLA" appeared on the scene and pulled to an abrupt stop. A cameraman leaped out onto the pavement like an acrobat. With camera attached to his shoulder, he focused on the rear door of the building.

Peter watched it all, dumbfounded. "They've got to know something I don't, that's for sure." Officers continued to arrive in every sort of patrol car imaginable. *Orange County Sheriff's Dept. Costa Mesa Police Department. Two unmarked cars.*

But for what? *Lord, if Angel is somehow involved in this, please be with her. Show her how to be the woman of God You've called her to be. Give her the strength and courage to do the right thing, even under tough circumstances. She needs a Damascus Road experience,*

Father, and if this is it, then open the eyes of her understanding.

A sudden sense of fear gripped him as he watched the scene unfold. What if Angel had to spend time in jail? He would visit her, of course. It would provide the perfect place for women from his church to minister to her one-on-one. *Lord, show me what to do, and I'll do it.*

Peter picked up his cell phone and dialed the church's number. Within minutes, he conveyed the whole story to Rob. What he knew of it, anyway.

Suddenly, from the rear door, several officers pressed their way out, ushering three men in handcuffs. The one in front had blond hair. The second one was short with curly dark hair and wire-rimmed glasses. The third. . .

The third man he knew quite well.

"No way." The cell phone slipped from his grasp. Peter watched in amazement as an armed officer led the tall dark-haired man to a patrol car and pushed him inside. A feeling of dread washed over him as he contemplated the possibilities.

He waited in silence until every last patrol car pulled away. Only then did he remember Rob remained on the other end of the line.

"You're not going to believe this," Peter said. "I hope you're sitting down."

fourteen

"Angel, are you ready?"

Angelina looked up from the makeup mirror into Mr. Nigel's anxious eyes. "Never more so, sir." She gave her face one last glance before standing. Eye makeup, good. Cheeks, fine. Lips. Oops, too much lipstick. She dabbed at them with a tissue and wheeled around for his stamp of approval.

Mr. Nigel patted her on the shoulder. "This is your chance to do what you've been trained to do. Go get 'em, tiger."

Angel's pulse sang in her ears. Sweat beaded on her upper lip. Years of preparation had led her here, and for the first time she felt the satisfaction of answering a God-given call. College professors had tried to dissuade her. Family members had attempted to redirect her. But Angel knew all along the Lord would give her the courage to perform the task. His Word promised it. "The one who is in you is greater than the one who is in the world." She kept the words from 1 John 4 in the back of her mind each day.

And this time, with God's help, she was ready—ready to face the people of Los Angeles. *This one's for you, Ida.*

A short time later, she stood before the camera, feeling lightheaded and giddy. For a brief moment panic struck her, and the burst of spiritual strength she had felt just moments before seemed to disappear. She thought she might be sick, but the wave of nausea passed. Angel cleared her throat, took a drink of water, and loosened up her shoulders and neck. *Greater is He that is in me.* She smiled confidently and winked at Mr. Nigel, who beamed like a proud papa.

The stage manager gave the prompting, "We're on in 3-2-1. . ."

The words "The Voice of the Angels" raced across the screen, accompanied by stylized angel wings. Angel watched it, mesmerized.

Then she was on. Though nervous, she spoke succinctly, assured of God's presence as every word streamed forth. "Here at KRLA we're hurt by the things that hurt you. Whenever we discover someone has been victimized, we want to be able to step in and do something. That's why, when sources tipped us off to an identity theft ring in Costa Mesa, we felt we had to do all we could to stop them in their tracks. These modern-day Robin Hoods seemed to be working in reverse—stealing from the poor and making themselves rich."

She shifted her position slightly as the stage manager directed.

"Their crime? Identity theft—the number one financial and consumer felony of the information age. Many people don't realize that identity theft is the fastest growing white-collar crime in the United States. According to statistics, this complicated offense has increased on average nearly forty percent per year with nearly one million people falling victim each year. The elderly are often targeted—in part because of their higher credit lines and good credit histories, and in part because they have greater home equity." Angel swallowed hard and steadied her voice. *Don't worry, Ida. You're going to get your home back.*

She forged ahead. "And let's not forget that the elderly are generally kinder and more compassionate. Ironically, this compassion makes them more gullible to believing lies. In short, they are often unaware of the evil that lurks around them. And identity theft is an evil business."

She grew more serious as she read the words she had written and rehearsed from the monitor. "Skilled thieves are often computer savvy and train for years in the arts of manipulation and thievery. Many have been found working in organized groups inside credit card companies, credit bureaus, banks, and even restaurants, where they frequently pose as computer technicians. Some use the Internet to con well-meaning people out of private information. Still others, less skilled perhaps, shoulder-surf at ATM machines or scavenge through trash cans, looking for carelessly tossed personal documents—anything with a bank account number, social security number, or credit card information. Those who have the necessary equipment even resort to printing and selling illegal social security cards."

She turned slightly to her left, letting her gaze follow the penetrating eye of the camera. "The suspected ring of thieves in Costa Mesa had managed to accomplish all of these things and then some. But they will have to sing their victory chant from behind bars at the Orange County jail." A tape began to roll. Familiar faces were ushered from Tennyson Towers in handcuffs.

"With KRLA's help," Angel continued, "the Costa Mesa police, along with the Orange County Sheriff's Department and agents from the FBI, have uncovered enough evidence to take the following men into custody—Nicholas Schuster of Riverside, Charles Banning of San Diego, Thomas Dempsey of Newport Beach, and Michael Grady of Anaheim. These four men have been charged with stealing nearly ten million dollars from unsuspecting Californians last year alone." A closeup of Nick's scowling face made her stomach churn, but she plowed ahead.

"Posing as an advertising firm, these would-be businessmen took up office at Tennyson Towers, a complex that houses more than a hundred legitimate businesses. They also managed to spend multiplied millions of dollars, purportedly on themselves, opening credit accounts at local stores, setting up cellular phone service, making hefty purchases over the Internet, and even booking lavish vacations for their families. All at someone else's expense."

Angel's heart swelled with excitement. "When KRLA first started working on this story, we had no way of knowing it would turn out to be the largest identity theft crime in California's history. Now that these men are behind bars, we feel confident we've made a difference."

As she glanced up at the monitor for one final peek at the footage, Angel's heart lurched. In the background, behind all the commotion, stood the familiar Dumpster. Cagey metal arms locked into the monstrosity and started to lift it. *Peter!*

The clip ended.

The camera zoomed in on Angel's face, and she forced herself to concentrate, though her voice now shook violently. She drove her nails into her palms. "Tha—that's what we're all about here at KRLA. We're on your side. If you have a story about someone in need or someone who's facing an obstacle they can't seem to overcome, feel free to give us a call or drop us an e-mail."

She took a deep breath, relieved to be nearing the end. "For tips on how you can avoid becoming a victim of identity theft, log onto our web site. For KRLA, this is Angelina Fuentes, the Voice of the Angels."

≈

"Peter!" a voice rang out across the large home. "Peter, get in here. Quick!"

Peter heard his mother's excited cries but couldn't seem to answer. He sat, locked in place, on the couch in the entertainment room.

She appeared in the doorway. "Did you see that?" She took a breath and plunged into the next sentence. "On the news! It was. . ."

"I saw it." Peter turned his attention back to the television screen, but the story had already changed. He couldn't believe what he had seen. And heard. Every word had proven Angel to be a saint, not the sinner he had made her out to be. Every crazy, wonderful word.

He turned back to face his mother. She couldn't seem to wipe the silly grin from her face, and for a minute Peter felt like joining her, though the joy he now felt was mixed with an odd sense of betrayal. Angel had been working undercover all along. Though he had suspected her of many things, that possibility had never entered his mind.

Her KRLA report had been worth the wait. For nearly an hour Peter had tried to keep from dozing on the couch as he contemplated the things he had seen and heard over the past week. After a glance at the evening news, he promised himself he would snatch a few moments of much-needed sleep. He certainly deserved it.

But curiosity held him captive. Something big had happened at the Towers this afternoon. Something that involved the police and that tall, dark-haired man Angel had run from on the fourth floor of Tennyson Towers.

And now he knew. Everything.

And nothing—all at the same time.

≈

Angel's shoulders slumped forward as the camera pulled away.

"You okay, sweetie?" Mr. Nigel appeared at her side.

"Yeah." She looked up into his kind eyes. "I'm just so relieved it's over. You have no idea."

"Sure I do." He wrapped an arm around her shoulder and gave her a fatherly squeeze. "But, girl, it's just beginning for you!" His face lit up. "There are other stories waiting in the wings. People need you—remember?"

"Oh! Speaking of which, I have a huge favor to ask you."

"Ask away. Your wish is my command."

Her heart surged with emotion. "Mr. Nigel, I want to meet Ida."

Her boss stared at her with a blank expression. "Who?"

"Ida. Davidson."

"Oh, uh. . .yeah." His looked at the floor and then ushered her to the side of the room. "Listen, Angel. There's something I need to tell you."

"Okay. But I really can't wait much longer to talk to her. I have so many ideas, so many plans for how we can help her."

Mr. Nigel pulled away and rubbed at his chin. "I, uh. . .I'm afraid that's going to be impossible."

"But why? We've done so much for her, and I know she'll want to meet me. Please, Mr. Nigel. Do this for me."

"Wish I could, Angel, but. . ." The color seemed to drain from his face. "You see, it's like this. Ida Davidson doesn't exist."

fifteen

Peter jammed his car into gear and breezed out onto the freeway. If everything went as planned, he could be at KRLA in forty-five minutes. Barring traffic, of course. He glanced at the digital clock. Six thirty-four. Surely the 405 would be emptying out by now.

Then again, this was Los Angeles.

He had to find Angel. Had to talk to her. More than anything, he needed to quiet the ache in his heart.

And slow down.

Peter carefully went back over the words in Angel's news report as he drove, trying to piece everything together. All of his former questions had been answered in one four-minute news segment.

And yet one lingering question remained. Could she forgive him?

As he pulled into the parking lot of KRLA, he prayed. *Lord, give me the right words. Don't let me blow this.* He quickly went through the dialogue in his head—what he would say when he saw her. How he would explain his bad behavior? How sorry he was, and how much he wanted and needed her forgiveness.

And then he would ask her out to dinner. If she would go, they'd have a wonderful conversation and laugh over the things they had been through in the past few days.

If.

Right now, he had to focus on finding her. Peter entered the lobby of KRLA.

"Hello?" he called out to an empty room. No response. He stepped through the double doors to his right. A tall, beefy-looking security guard dressed in a black uniform stopped him in his tracks. "Where do you think you're going?"

The man's gravelly voice sounded intimidating. Peter drew in a deep breath and looked up at him. "I, uh, I'm looking for someone."

The security guard crossed his arms. "Do your looking tomorrow before five." He took a step in Peter's direction.

"But this place is open all night, right? I mean, you've got another news show in just a few hours."

"We're not open to the public after five o'clock. And certainly not to someone who won't take no for an answer." The man took another step toward him.

"I'm looking for one of your reporters," Peter explained, backing up. "I'm pretty sure she's still here because I just saw her on the news."

"Uh-huh. And who might that be?"

He shuffled his keys from his right hand to his left. "Angel. Angelina Fuentes. She's a—a friend of mine."

The guy's expression changed immediately. "Oh, you know Angel?" At Peter's nod his face lit fully. "That girl is something else. She sure did herself proud today, didn't she? Not to mention making the rest of us here at the station proud."

Peter nodded numbly.

"Well, you just missed her. They took her out to celebrate."

"They?"

"Mr. Nigel and the others," the security guard said. "Don't

have a clue where they went, though. Hey, what did you say your name was again?"

"Peter. Peter Campbell." He shook the security guard's hand and breathed a sigh of relief. "Do you think she'll be back tonight?"

"Nah. Not till Monday." At Peter's downcast face, he added, "Looks like you'll have the whole weekend to think about her." He looked Peter in the eye. "Pretty hung up on her, huh?"

"I, uh. . ." Peter stammered as his gaze shifted to the floor. "Yeah. Yeah, I guess I am."

❧

"Great job, Angel!" Voices rang out in the crowded restaurant as congratulations were passed around. Angel drank it all in, content in the fact that she had completed her task successfully. And survived.

As the crew of KRLA met together for the celebratory dinner, she couldn't help but feel a sense of somber satisfaction, but she was still a little frustrated at Mr. Nigel for lying to her about Ida. And she was anxious to know what project lay around the bend. What did he have in mind for her next story?

Now's as good a time as any to ask. She leaned over and whispered the question, hoping she would not be overheard. "Where do we go from here?"

"Home, I guess." He yawned.

"No, sir. I mean, what's next for me at KRLA? What sort of story did you have in mind? And how often will I do the Voice of the Angels segment? Once a day? Once a week?"

"Whoa! Slow down, girl!"

Angel caught her breath. "I don't want to seem ungrateful,

but I'm so ready to take on a new project. I love helping people, Mr. Nigel. I feel like I was born for this job."

He patted her on the arm. "I know, kid. You're our angel." He paused for a moment. "We'll start with a story a week. Then, as ideas start flowing, we'll look at a daily bit. Speaking of ideas, something we talked about over the phone this morning triggered an idea."

"Really?" Angel sat up straight in her chair.

"That blond guy. The one you thought was involved in the identity theft ring—"

"Peter Campbell?"

"Yeah. That guy. Remember I told you about some feeding center he works at down there in Costa Mesa? They provide meals for the homeless, that sort of thing."

"Right, right."

"They've also got a street church of some sort, but I heard they're understaffed and underpaid. In need of community support, from what I've been told. Might make an interesting human-interest piece. Anything you might report could help raise funds to feed people who might not get a meal otherwise."

"Sounds great." She contemplated his words. "I guess I should go out there and look the place over then." Her heartbeat quickened at the thought of seeing Peter again.

"Yep. Their office opens at nine on Monday. Here's the address." He handed her a card and then leaned back in his chair with a long yawn.

Angel shook her head in disbelief. "You had this planned all along."

"I did." He gave her a wicked grin. "But no hurry, sweetie. Take a couple of days off to enjoy your success. It is the weekend, after all."

❧

The next morning Angel rose bright and early. *I know it's not Monday, but I can't wait that long. Besides, there's got to be some sort of activity going on at that feeding center today. Wouldn't hurt to stop in for a quick peek.* She looked through her wardrobe for just the right outfit, finally settling on a white cotton blouse and a pair of her most comfortable jeans. As she headed for the door, she couldn't help but think about Peter Campbell.

Lord, he's everything he made himself out to be, and I never even gave him a chance. Help me to find him, and I'll try to make everything right.

"Where are you off to?" Her mother's voice rang out across the spacious foyer just as Angel opened the front door.

She turned, trying to hide her broad smile. "Back to Costa Mesa, Mom."

Her mother looked at her suspiciously. "And?"

"Don't worry. It's not what you're thinking."

"With a look like that on your face, there's only one thing I'm thinking." Her mother's expression changed to one of sheer relief, and she clasped her hands together in excitement. "You're going to see him again, aren't you?"

"See who?" Angel wound a strand of hair around her finger.

"You know who. That guy your brother told me about. Peter something-or-other."

Nardo. You never could keep a secret. She should have known. "Peter Campbell?" She shifted her purse from one shoulder to another and played innocent. "I, uh. . . I might run into him. I'm going down to a feeding center in Costa Mesa. He does work there sometimes."

"He works with the homeless?" Her mother's face lit up. At Angel's nod, she said, "Doesn't get much better than that. Go get him, honey."

Angel laughed as she headed out the door. In fact, she couldn't seem to wipe the goofy smile from her face all the way to Costa Mesa. As she pulled up to the feeding center, her nerves suddenly kicked in.

A group of teens, dressed in identical T-shirts, met her outside the front door. "Hey, aren't you that lady?" one of them called out.

"Yeah," another added. "The one on the news last night."

"Angel Fuentes." She extended her hand.

"Cool. I'm shaking hands with an angel," the boy said with a grin. "Don't think I'll ever wash this hand again." He held it up for the approval of his friends, who looked genuinely amused. "Wait'll I tell my friends at church."

"Speaking of church," Angel said, "is there some sort of service going on here this morning? Looks like a lot of activity for a Saturday."

"Just the usual Sidewalk Sunday School for the street kids—even though it's Saturday."

"Ah, I see."

"We usually just call it Kids' Church," the boy explained. "We do a service for the kids and then feed them lunch. Some of them wouldn't get to eat otherwise." A moment of silence passed between them before he extended his hand. "I'm Sam Bradley. This is Megan Johnson. A group of us come down from our church every Saturday to help with the kids. We do dramas and stuff."

"Cool." Angel smiled. "Anyone else from your church come?" She bit her lip in anticipation of his answer.

"Yeah." He shrugged. "A bunch of people."

She drew in a deep breath. "Would Peter Campbell be one of those people?" She couldn't hide her grin.

The boy's eyebrows elevated. "You know Peter?"

"Yes."

His eyes lit up, and he began to talk with his hands as he spoke. "Peter's like my big brother. Spiritually, anyway. Sort of a mentor, you know?" All of the teens began to chatter at once, extolling Peter's virtues and looking her over with renewed interest.

"Will he be here today?" she asked.

"He's here every Saturday," Megan said. "Usually sits up front with the three- and four-year-olds." Even as she spoke the words, the place began to fill with kids.

"We've got to go now," Sam called out as they walked toward the door. "Hope you can stay for the service. We could use some help with the kids."

Angel stayed for the entire service, amazed at how many children showed up. At least two hundred, maybe more. The teens led the group in some lively praise and worship and played games with them. Then they performed a drama that kept the children captivated. By the time the service ended, she knew she had to write a story about this place. How could she not?

Even if she hadn't seen the one person she came to see.

She needed to find him, needed to explain everything. Too many unspoken words lingered in the air between them. Her emotions wouldn't allow her to wait much longer, though she had fought against her feelings all morning.

Should she go to his house? Would that be too forward? Would he even speak to her? Somehow she couldn't escape the vision of his beautiful eyes. Her heart wouldn't let her forget.

Peter Campbell is an amazing man of God. But in order to tell him, she had to find him.

sixteen

Peter spent Sunday afternoon dialing every Fuentes in the book. His persistence paid off at 5:16 p.m. "Could I speak to Angel, please?"

"Is this Peter?" An excited female voice greeted him, one that sounded a little like Angel's, only perhaps older.

"Yes." He nearly dropped the receiver.

The woman's words seemed rushed. "This is Consuela Fuentes, Angelina's mother. I'm so happy to speak with you." She spoke rapidly with a rich Spanish accent, and he strained to understand every single word.

"Um, you, too."

"You're Angel's young man, aren't you?"

"I, uh, I am?"

"I heard all about you from my son, Nardo. I believe he drove our Angel to your house not too long ago."

Nardo? The guy in the car was her brother? Just one more piece to the puzzle.

"When are we going to meet you?" The woman spoke with such excitement it terrified him. And gave him hope.

He swallowed and forged ahead. "Well, I don't know. I was hoping to speak to Angel, actually."

"Oh, my. Angelina went out to lunch with friends after church," Mrs. Fuentes explained.

Church. She goes to church. He breathed a huge sigh of relief as the woman continued on.

"Then I know she had some sort of meeting about the new college and career Bible study group she's starting."

"She's leading a Bible study?"

"Oh, yes," Mrs. Fuentes said. "Something from the book of James, I think. At any rate, she won't be home until after the service tonight."

"Okay. Well, thank you very much."

"Why don't I give you our address, and you can come by sometime?"

He reached for a pen, nearly knocking the phone book off the table in the process. "That would be nice."

She gave him the address and wished him well, then signed off with a click. As Peter dropped the phone onto the kitchen counter, he couldn't help but grin. The Lord had apparently seen fit to give him a second chance. This time he wouldn't blow it.

☙

The next morning, Peter dressed for work as usual. However, he had a stop to make on the way to Costa Mesa. He would go by Angel's place on the way—if, in fact, it proved to be on the way.

He looked up the address on the Internet. Bel-Air West? The neighborhood was far north of Newport Beach and completely in the opposite direction. Still, if he hurried, he might be able to at least swing by. . .

All Peter wanted was just a glimpse of Angel. It would be too early to wake her, but maybe, just maybe, he would catch her leaving for work. Then he would summon the courage to speak to her—to explain, to apologize.

If he made it there. He glanced at the clock once again: 7:13 a.m.

As he drove through traffic, he couldn't help but wonder if he had made a mistake in attempting this feat so early in the day. Not only would it cause him to be late for work, he'd barely have time to say two words to Angel if he did happen to see her.

And yet something wouldn't let him turn the car around. By the time he reached Mulholland, the sun shone brightly. Peter glanced at his watch and groaned. He should be starting his rounds right now. He made a quick call to explain his tardiness and found a sympathetic ear on the other end of the phone. *Thank You, Lord.*

As Peter pulled into Angel's subdivision, a revelation hit him. All this time he had thought of her as poverty-stricken. It never occurred to him that she might be from a well-to-do family. But the homes in this subdivision certainly attested to that fact. A sense of dread filled him almost immediately. *If she's from a wealthy family, why would she be interested in a trash collector?*

He very nearly turned the car around. Only one thing prevented it. Rob's sermon yesterday morning had struck a nerve. One passage in particular had forced Peter to take a look at his own shortcomings and weigh them against his actions over the past several months. The verse from Proverbs stayed with him—all through the night, in fact. "A man's pride brings him low, but a man of lowly spirit gains honor."

For months Peter had claimed to avoid his father's brand of pride—the sort that puffed itself up. Instead, without even realizing it, he had substituted his own version. "Anything that causes you to focus on yourself is pride," Rob had preached. "Arrogance is one form, yes, but one form only.

Thinking too little of yourself is another. Anything that places your eyes on yourself could be labeled pride."

Interesting revelation. And here he sat, facing the very truth of those words. This time, the truth carried a sting he had not expected. Laying aside all pride meant it shouldn't make any difference—whether he worked as a trash collector or a well-paid talent agent. It also shouldn't matter if Angel came from a life of poverty or a life of luxury. If God had truly brought them together, the only real concerns were issues of the heart.

Even now, his heart felt as if it would burst inside him each time he thought about Angel. What was it he had said to Rob just a few short days ago? *The woman I have in mind for my wife will be ministry-oriented. She'll be sweet and kind and have a heart for the down-and-out. She'll be someone who lives to help people, not steal from them.*

"*I see your dilemma,*" Rob had responded. "*The girl you've described is nothing like that.*"

Peter shook his head in disbelief. "How wrong could I be?"

He pulled his car to a stop in front of a white brick house and prayed for the courage to face the woman he had waited for all his life.

⋙

Angel turned her car into the parking lot at Tennyson Towers. She had come with one purpose in mind—to wait for Peter Campbell. She would sit in her car until the trash truck arrived. Then she would do what she had longed to do for days. She would offer him an apology and an explanation. Next she would ask if they could start over again—from the very beginning. He would forgive her and, for old time's sake, she would take him to lunch at the same little diner he had introduced her to that first day. Then she would ask him to go with her to the feeding center, where she would meet with the director and begin her next story. Peter would assist her.

Yes, she certainly had every detail worked out. Except one. How to find Peter. She waited awhile longer, glancing at her watch on occasion: 9:32 a.m. *Probably a little early.* No matter. She would sit here as long as it took.

Angel pulled a stick of gum out of her purse and popped it in her mouth. Then she turned on the radio. *A talk show? No thanks. I need something that will keep me awake.* She yawned and switched stations. When the strains of a familiar love song filled the car, she leaned back against the seat and relaxed.

Why do I still dream of you?
Why are you the one I long for?

Her heart overflowed. *Lord, I know I don't know Peter very well, but You've brought us together for some reason. Don't let me lose him now. Please, Lord.*

She replayed every time she had seen Peter Campbell over the past week, smiling with each memory.

His face as he reached to help her out of the Dumpster.

His smile as she ordered enough food for two people at the diner.

His look of compassion as he laid out the gospel message while she waited for her brother's car to arrive.

His wide-eyed stare as she entered his home dressed in that new black dress.

His look of sheer terror and confusion as she ran from the office on the fourth floor.

All of these surfaced, and more. Angel pushed down the emotions that accompanied the memories, forcing herself not to cry as she thought about what a good man he had turned out to be. *I was so wrong about him, but I'll make it up to him. I will.*

Her reflections slowed and memories of yesterday's meeting at church surfaced. In spite of her heavy workload at KRLA, Angel had another project in mind. She would soon head up a Bible study on the book of James. In preparation, God had revealed so many things to her from His Word.

She reached for her Bible and opened it to the first chapter of James. Angel couldn't help but smile as she read, "Consider it pure joy, my brothers, whenever you face trials of many kinds, because you know that the testing of your faith develops perseverance. Perseverance must finish its work so that you may be mature and complete, not lacking anything."

The past week had certainly tried her patience. She had nearly given up on several occasions. But perseverance was finishing its work, and she was rapidly on her way to becoming complete.

seventeen

Peter summoned up the courage to knock on the front door
of the Fuentes home, but no one answered. For some time
he stood there, waiting. Feeling dejected, he climbed back
into his car and leaned his head against the steering wheel.
Would he and Angel ever see each other again, or was
he just trying to force the Lord's hand? As he turned the
key in the ignition, he analyzed the situation a bit more
clearly. He had wasted a trip into the city and risked his job
in the process.

All the way back to Costa Mesa, he prayed God would
show him what his next move should be. If any.

❧

11:14 a.m.

Angel squirmed as she waited. Finally, when she could
take it no more, she climbed out of the car and headed
toward the building.

A chill ran up her spine as she opened the back door
of Tennyson Towers. To think, just a few short days ago
she had fled through this very door. On that day this
place had terrified her. Today it seemed just an ordinary
office complex.

Angel's heels clicked as she made her way across the
lobby. She entered the ladies' room and quickly headed for a
stall. On her way out, she gave her appearance a once-over
in the mirror. "Hmmm." She pulled a tube of lipstick from

her purse and touched up her lips. She stepped back and took a look at herself.

Today's apparel was quite different from anything she had worn last week. The tailored tan suit complemented her dark hair, and the cream-colored blouse looked almost white against her olive skin. She had swept her hair up with a clip and carefully applied makeup and nail polish. She wore a silver necklace with a delicate cross pendant around her neck—a gift from her parents last Christmas. Today Angel wasn't playing a part. Today she was just herself.

As she turned to leave, the bathroom door opened, and a woman shuffled inside with a mop in her hands. "Oh, excuse me, honey, I didn't know anyone was in here." The older woman turned, then looked back and gazed at her curiously. "Hey, aren't you—?"

Angel extended her hand. "We've never been properly introduced. My name is Angel Fuentes."

"The Voice of the Angels." The older woman grinned. "I saw you on the news. We all did." She paused as she gave Angel a funny look. "Answered a lot of questions in my mind, if you don't mind my saying so."

"I'm glad," Angel said. "I suppose we do need to talk, don't we?"

"Yes. Well, I thought it was you, honey," Mabel said, "but to be honest, you look so different all done up like that, I hardly knew you. Quite a difference from the girl I met last week."

"I owe you an apology," Angel said. "I'm really sorry I couldn't tell you who I was. You see, I—"

"Don't say another word." Mabel put both hands in the air in mock despair. "You don't owe me a thing. In fact, we probably owe you. If you hadn't stopped those guys upstairs, who knows what might have become of all of us?"

"I wasn't trying to be deceptive, especially not to you."

"Oh, forget it, hon. I might be old, but I still love a little adventure." She grinned like a schoolgirl. "What brings you back out here today? Not more bad news, I hope."

"Oh, no. Nothing like that. You see, I, uh, well. . ."

"Another escapade?" Mabel's eyes lit up.

Angel shrugged. "Of a different sort, maybe. You see, there's this guy. I met him last week."

"Oooh! A romantic adventure! Well, out with it, kid. I don't have all day." Mabel leaned against the counter and listened as Angel shared the story of how Peter had found her in the Dumpster that very first day. The older woman nodded several times as the story continued. When the whole story was finished, she said, "I have just one question for you, honey. What in the world are you doing in here talking to this old lady when you could be out there, making things right with the man of your dreams?"

Angel glanced at her watch again. "Oh, no!" She gave Mabel a quick hug, then raced from the bathroom back out into the lobby. Through the glass door she could see the Dumpster in the back parking lot. She made her way outside and walked over to see if it had been emptied.

Full.

Angel fought to catch her breath. She looked up as she heard Mabel's voice. "Didn't miss him, did you?"

"No. Thank goodness."

"Well, why don't you wait over here on the bench? I was

just about to take my lunch break." She waved a paper bag. "How does ham and cheese on wheat sound to you?"

"Great," Angel said. "I'm starving." She followed Mabel to the comfort of the bench. *This is the very spot where Peter tried to witness to me.*

As they sat, Mabel shared her views on love, on youth, and on faith. Angel listened carefully, nibbling on the much-needed sandwich. When she glanced at her watch again, she was surprised to see how quickly the time had flown. 12:33 p.m. "Well, I hate to cut this short, but I've got a one-o'clock appointment." She stood to her feet and stretched, suddenly realizing how tired she was. The events of the past week were catching up with her.

"You're going to miss him, honey!" Mabel said.

"I don't know what else to do. I'm supposed to meet with the director at the feeding center at one. I'm working on a new story for the station."

"Well, I'll be praying for you, then." Mabel stood and wrapped her arms around Angel. "In the meantime, I'd better get myself back to work before they can me." She waved as she entered the building. "See you on television."

Angel waved her response, then quickly finished the sandwich and ate a couple of potato chips. With a sigh, she wadded up the paper bag and napkin. She walked toward the Dumpster with trash in hand, deep in thought, and tossed the bag over the top of the Dumpster.

Back at her car she tried to open the door but found it locked. *Oh, I forgot. . . .* She fished around in her pocket for the keys. *Where did I put them? They were right here, in my. . .hand. They were in my hand. I had them in my hand with the bag. And now the bag is—*

She looked back at the Dumpster defeated. *Don't tell me.* She leaned against the car.

"I'll have to call Nardo again. He'll come and get me." But how? Her cell phone sat on the front seat in plain view. Locked in.

Angel groaned as she made her way toward the Dumpster again. She recoiled at the foul odor coming from inside.

An opening on the backside of the Dumpster beckoned. At least she wouldn't have to climb over this time. Maybe she could just lean inside a bit and have a peek. Surely the keys would reveal themselves.

Angel leaned in and quickly found herself dangling over the edge by her midsection. She wiggled her way inside, pinching her nose and squealing. "This is so gross!" She screamed as her hand grasped something slimy. Chinese food. She rubbed it against her thigh, leaving a dark stain on her pants. Then she pressed forward in the quest for her keys.

She heard voices as people walked by and quickly slid the side panel closed, hoping not to be discovered. *I'll get out of here on my own. As soon as I can find those keys, that is.* The minutes ticked away as she grabbed at anything and everything that resembled a set of keys. Finally she located them. Under her left foot. She must have accidentally stepped on the panic button because, from across the parking lot, her car alarm went off. Angel grabbed the remote and pressed the button, but the keys slipped through her fingers again. Down they went, somewhere between the Chinese food and an open container of yogurt.

She stuck one hand down and grasped for them. This time

she held on with a vengeance and snapped the alarm off. She waded back over to the side of the Dumpster and pulled at the side panel to open it.

It wouldn't budge.

eighteen

God, have I missed You completely? Peter prayed all the way to Costa Mesa. *Every time I turn around, I think I'm doing Your will, but then things don't turn out the way I think they're going to. Am I completely off base?*

He felt almost sick as he thought about Angel. His misconceptions of her had caused a huge rift between them, one that might never be mended. And yet it must be mended. He knew in his heart that meeting her had been no accident. Surely the Lord had a bigger plan. Peter's heart wouldn't hurt this badly, otherwise.

As he turned onto Harbor Boulevard, his thoughts shifted to the relationship with his father once again. He still hadn't worked up the courage to approach his dad for a heart-to-heart discussion about their relationship.

But he would do that tonight. The relationship with his father could be mended. Would be mended.

But the relationship with Angel. . .

That would take an act of God.

❧

You've got to be kidding me. Angel tugged again and again at the metal panel until her strength gave out. Frustrated, she stood to grasp the top rim. *Looks like I'm going to have to get out of here the hard way.* As she pulled herself up, she heard the sickening sound of brakes squealing, coupled with an engine's roar. "No!" The shriek of grinding metal came next.

Suddenly the Dumpster jolted. Angel thought her heart would lurch from her chest as she peered over the edge of the Dumpster and found herself face-to-face with the trash truck once again. "No! Peter! Peter, stop!" She screamed as loudly as she could, but the noises kept him from looking her way.

She caught his attention just as the monstrous contraption tipped forward. Peter's eyes grew large as they locked into hers. His mouth flew open. The Dumpster stopped immediately and rocked back and forth, suspended in space. Angel lost her grip on the edge and lurched backwards. The keys flew out of her hand once again.

Iron thrashed against iron. She heard it all and instinctively knew what would come next. The arms released the Dumpster. It hit the ground with a thud, and she found herself immersed in garbage from toe to eyebrow. She sighed and began to pick chow mein noodles out of her hair.

"Angel?" Peter's voice rang out from the parking lot. "Angel, I'm so sorry. Are you okay?" He sounded terrified.

She groaned and leaned back against the edge of the Dumpster in defeat. "I'm fine. Just get me out of here!"

He leaped over the top of the Dumpster and flattened a tub of sweet and sour sauce with his backside as he landed. It sprayed everywhere. Angel couldn't help but laugh.

"Oh, you think that's funny?" he grinned.

"Well, yeah."

"Pretty humorous, coming from someone with Chinese food in her hair." He reached out to touch her hair, and Angel's stomach flip-flopped.

His hand paused as it brushed her cheek. "You've got a little something right here." He dabbed at something just under her right eye. Angel reached up with a sticky hand to grab hold of his. "Peter, I have to talk to you." She squeezed his hand until the ache in her heart began to cease. "There's so much I need to tell you. So much I—"

He smiled. "You don't have to say anything."

"But I have to. You don't understand."

"You don't have to say anything else, Angelina Fuentes."

She let go of his hand immediately. "You know my name?"

"You are the Voice of the Angels, aren't you?" He gave her a goofy grin.

She buried her head into sticky palms and groaned. "Yes. I mean, that's what they call me, anyway. But I'm no angel. At least I haven't been where you're concerned. I'm pretty sure you think I'm just awful."

"I wouldn't be so sure about that. In fact, I think I see a halo right over here." He pointed at something shimmering behind her.

"My keys!"

"Yep." He reached to pick them up.

"Looks like you've saved me." Angel's voice softened as she added, "Again."

"No. I don't think so." He suddenly looked embarrassed. "I'd have to say this time you saved me." He extended his hand in her direction.

"What do you mean?" She took the keys but refused to let go of his hand. She might never let go again.

"All my life, I've prided myself on not being prideful," he said. "Then I had to go and meet someone like you—someone who lives to help others." Peter's gaze shifted downward.

"Me?" She gasped. "What about you? You work at that

feeding center. You take care of those children."

His cheeks flushed. "How did you know all of that?"

A sudden burst of laughter unified them for one crazy moment, but it ended suddenly. Immediately, Angel knew what would happen next. They moved awkwardly toward one another and gently brushed lips in a shy kiss. When they pulled apart, Angel saw tears forming in his eyes. *God, is it really possible? Is this why You've led me here?*

Peter wrapped a sticky arm around her neck and drew her close for a kiss that settled any unanswered questions in her mind.

Father, are You really this good? Do I deserve someone so angelic?

Peter loosened his hold on her slightly. "I don't deserve you," he whispered.

"What? Oh, Peter." She planted tender kisses on his damp lashes, then traced the tearstains down to his lips once again.

"But I misjudged you," he whispered. "I thought you were—" He couldn't seem to make himself say the words.

"A liar?"

"Well, yeah. And a little more." He paused. "Angel, I've been falling in love with you for a week, and I didn't even know your true identity. Is that crazy?"

"Did you say falling in love?" He nodded, and she reached for his hand. "Peter, I'm so sorry I couldn't let you know the real me. I didn't mean to deceive you. I was just. . .stuck."

"I know. . . ." He gently touched her cheek with the back of his hand.

"You know what?"

"Angel, I don't know any other way to say this, so I'm just going to say it."

She held her breath and waited.

"I know that God has brought us together for a reason," he said finally.

"Agreed."

"And on some level we've both been rescued this week. Me from my pride and you from those guys up on the fourth floor."

She groaned. "I can't believe I thought you actually worked for them."

"I can't believe I thought you were a criminal. One of the prettiest criminals I've ever met, by the way. Just in case I haven't said it before."

Angel felt her cheeks flush. He reached to plant a light kiss on each one, then took her hand. "What do you say we get out of here and find someplace to get cleaned up? I think it's time you and I had a good, long talk."

nineteen

Peter's heart raced as the makeup crew plastered pancake makeup all over his face. He sneezed as a layer of powder went on top. "Are you sure all of this is necessary?" He gave himself a once-over in the mirror and groaned. "It's just a two-minute segment."

"It's necessary, trust me." Angel spoke from the chair next to his. "Better get used to it. With as much community service as you do, you'll probably end up on the news a lot." She winked, and his heart melted, as always.

"Now that I have my own personal reporter, you mean?" *How much more could I ask for?*

The woman he loved looked over with a shrug and took his hand. He gave it a squeeze. Then he sat in silence, listening to the sound of her voice as she gave instructions to the cameraman. She radiated self-assurance. Her voice, her poise, her gentle assertions—they all amazed and delighted him.

For several months, Peter and Angel had grown to know one another, truly know one another. Their love had surpassed anything he could have hoped or prayed for. God had surprised him with the love of his life.

And now, on the day the City of Costa Mesa had chosen to honor him publicly for his community service, he had a little surprise of his own.

⁂

Angel felt a tap on her shoulder and turned immediately.

"Oh, Peter. You startled me."

"Sorry." His hands trembled slightly as he took hold of hers.

"Are you okay? Not nervous, are you?" She wrapped her arm around his waist and laid her head on his chest.

"Um, a little."

That would explain the pounding chest. "First time on TV?" She looked up to gauge his response.

His face lit up. "I was almost in a peanut butter commercial once."

"Almost?" He was full of stories. "Peter, you're funny."

"No, really. I didn't do it because I was too scared. But my dad is happy I'm finally making my television debut." He grinned.

"So, you told him?"

"Yep. He'll be watching. Said he's taping it."

Angel knew how wonderful Peter felt about the new improvements in the relationship with his father. They had prayed about it almost from the beginning of their own relationship.

"Well, it won't be long now." She glanced at her watch. "We're on in just a few minutes."

"I know." His shaking intensified, and Angel wondered if he might be sick.

"There is this one little thing I need to take care of first," he said.

He turned the other way, and for a brief moment Angel thought he might flee the room. *Is he really that scared?* She reached out to touch his arm. "I don't know if you'll have time right now. Can it wait?"

"Nope. 'Fraid not."

Lord, help him. Please.

He turned back toward her. In his hand he held a tiny box, wrapped in silver paper with a delicate gold bow.

"What's this?" she whispered.

"For you."

She took it with some confusion. "It's not even Christmas yet," she pouted. "Besides, I don't have your gift."

"We're on in four minutes," the stage manager whispered into her headset. Angel nodded and turned her attention back to Peter.

He shrugged. "This is just a little something I picked up awhile back. Thought you could use it now."

"Right now?" He nodded, and she quickly opened the box and pulled out a delicate glass angel. "Oh, it's so pretty. Where did you get this?"

"At a shop in Laguna." He bit his lip. "I thought maybe you could hang it on your tree."

"I love angels!"

"I know. Me, too." He grinned mischievously and drew her close.

"Thank you so much." She reached to plant tiny kisses on his face, then lifted the tiny glass figure up for a closer look. "She's beautiful."

"So is this Angel." Peter leaned in for a kiss that almost knocked her off her feet. She wrapped her arms around his neck and gave herself over to the moment.

The stage manager interrupted their privacy with another hoarse whisper. "Three minutes."

Angel quickly pulled away from Peter and pressed the ornament back in the box. "Thanks for the gift," she whispered. "I owe you."

He took the box, reopened it, and held the glass cherub

up once again. Angel felt herself growing a little impatient with him. "What are you doing, Peter? We're about to go on."

"For an investigative reporter, you're sure not very good at scoping out the details." He twirled it around close to her face.

"What do you mean?"

His eyes twinkled. "Have another look."

Angel glanced at the angel again but noticed nothing unusual.

"Two minutes," the stage manager whispered.

"Her halo is a little smaller than yours," Peter said with a smile. "And it's probably a little looser, too."

Angel looked down at the tiny gold halo and noticed for the first time the sparkling stones lining the front. The shimmer of the center stone caused her heart to leap, and Angel realized in one moment what she had missed all along.

"You see," Peter said, as he untied a tiny white ribbon and loosed the ring, "I thought my Angel could use a little embellishment." The corners of his lips turned up as he held the engagement ring on the tip of his index finger for her approval. "If she'll have me, that is." He dropped to his knee and reached for her hand. Around her, people began to stir. Anxious eyes glanced their way. "Will you, Angel?"

The stage manager's voice interrupted her thoughts with his crisp instructions. "One minute. Take your places, please."

Angel could hardly catch her breath. "Oh, Peter."

"Is that your final answer?" He frowned.

"No! I mean, yes!" she squealed. "Yes, I'll marry you." The studio erupted into spontaneous applause.

God, is this really possible? She watched as Peter slipped the ring on her finger then stood to wrap her in his arms.

Every good and perfect gift is from above, coming down from the Father of the heavenly lights, who does not change like shifting shadows. Where the scripture came from, she had no idea.

Ah, yes. The book of James. First chapter. God did indeed have a sense of humor.

The lights overhead came on, nearly blinding her. She and Peter took their mark. He reached to kiss her once again, and she lost all track of time. The show didn't matter. The story didn't matter. All that mattered was the two of them. The lights grew brighter still, and Angel pulled back to look into Peter's eyes. Like her own, they were full of tears.

Funny, with the light streaming through his blond hair like that, he looked almost like. . .

Nah. He was just a man. But what a man. And what a miracle the Lord had seen fit to share him with her.

"I love you," she whispered as she reached to wipe away fresh tears.

"I love you more." He squeezed her hand in response. The stage manager spoke his final instructions as Angel and Peter locked hands and hearts. "You're on in three, two, one. . ."

Together, they turned to face the light.

A Letter To Our Readers

Dear Reader:

In order that we might better contribute to your reading enjoyment, we would appreciate your taking a few minutes to respond to the following questions. We welcome your comments and read each form and letter we receive. When completed, please return to the following:

Fiction Editor
Heartsong Presents
PO Box 719
Uhrichsville, Ohio 44683

1. Did you enjoy reading *Angel Incognito* by Janice Thompson?
   ❏ Very much! I would like to see more books by this author!
   ❏ Moderately. I would have enjoyed it more if

   _____

   _____

   _____

2. Are you a member of **Heartsong Presents**? ❏ Yes ❏ No
   If no, where did you purchase this book? _____

   _____

3. How would you rate, on a scale from 1 (poor) to 5 (superior), the cover design? _____

4. On a scale from 1 (poor) to 10 (superior), please rate the following elements.

   ____ Heroine   ____ Plot
   ____ Hero   ____ Inspirational theme
   ____ Setting   ____ Secondary characters

5. These characters were special because? _____

_____

_____

6. How has this book inspired your life? _____

_____

_____

7. What settings would you like to see covered in future
   Heartsong Presents books? _____

_____

_____

8. What are some inspirational themes you would like to see
   treated in future books? _____

_____

_____

9. Would you be interested in reading other **Heartsong
   Presents** titles? ❏ Yes ❏ No

10. Please check your age range:
    ❏ Under 18   ❏ 18-24
    ❏ 25-34   ❏ 35-45
    ❏ 46-55   ❏ Over 55

Name _____

Occupation _____

Address _____

City_____ State_____ Zip_____